MESSAGE in the BLOOD

Dawn Merriman

Copyright © 2022 Dawn Merriman
All rights reserved.
ISBN-13: 9798834932369

Dedication

This book is dedicated to my wonderful husband, Kevin and my children. Thank you for always supporting me. Also dedicated to Carlie Frech, Belinda Martin and Katie Hoffman for pushing me to finish and for all the insights and encouragement.

-Dawn Merriman

Chapter 1

LACEY ANISTON

The roof of my mouth is burned from the hot cheese of the pizza I ate earlier. I rub my tongue across the rough flesh and finish off my glass of wine in an attempt to cool the scorch. The sweet liquid cools my mouth, but does little to stop the wave of anxiety sizzling beneath the surface. I smooth my hand over my no longer grumbling stomach and look for the hundredth time out the front window of my apartment. I hope to see my sister, Aubry, hurrying up the sidewalk. I can imagine her coming to my door, her overlarge purse bumping against her legs.

I squint and I can see her.

I open my eyes and the sidewalk is empty. As I watch, a scrap of paper blows across the vacant concrete, dances in the air.

I pour another glass of wine, but leave it untouched next to the half-empty pizza box.

I'd waited for my sister, Aubry, to come over as we planned and help me eat it, but she never showed. It wasn't like her to miss our usual Sunday night dinner at my apartment. It was one of the few things I looked forward to during the week. When she was late, my grumbling stomach got the better of me and I reheated the delivered pizza in the microwave. The extra pepperoni, extra cheese, extra sauce deliciousness is another weekly indulgence relegated to Sundays. As a woman who makes her living in front of a camera, I have to be careful about what crosses my lips. My pizza dinners with my sister give me the strength to face the carrot sticks and salads the rest of the week.

By the time I finished off the third piece and checked my phone for the twenty-fourth time for an answer to my texts to Aubry more than the roof of my mouth is aching.

I know something is wrong.

My fingers furiously type another text. "I'm not kidding around now. Either get back to me or I'm coming over. If Brent is behind this, I'll kill him."

I stab the phone and send the text. Before the phone can whoosh the send sound I'm on my feet and reaching for my purse.

Aubry has never missed a Sunday dinner with me without calling first and letting me know. In all the world, she is the one person I trust most. The one person I would never expect to stand me up.

If Brent is behind it, I swear....

I swear what? I've warned her before, and it has led nowhere. What can I do besides warn her that I know what he's done to her. Tell her to leave? Beg her to come live with me?

For a shiny moment, I imagine Aubry living with me. Another person to fill the emptiness of my apartment, of my life. Anyone. I'd love to have anyone. When my young son went to live with his dad permanently, it left a hole in my heart.

I start the car, roll down the window a few inches and light a cigarette. The smoke bites the back of my throat and the nicotine rushes my blood, mixes with the pizza I over-ate and the two glasses of wine.

As I drive to Aubry's apartment, I will my phone to ring, to chirp, to do anything to let me know she's okay.

I know she's not.

Sometimes I just know things. I don't want to be able to, but there you have it.

I suck down the cigarette and toss it out the window just as I turn onto Aubry's street. I park behind Aubry's Prius and look up at the house. The three story home was lovely in a previous life, now it has been chopped into four different apartments. Aubry's is the basement level, windows peek into the flower beds. The whole house is dark except one dim light glimmering from deep inside her apartment.

I wish I had come earlier, before the spring sun dipped below the horizon. The looming house gives off an energy I'd rather not face.

I want another cigarette and I'm not sure what to do now that I'm here. Brent's truck is parked in front of Aubry's Prius, so both of them are home, presumably. If they are having some sort of lover's spat, she won't want me to get into the middle of it, but I will.

If he's laying hands on my sister again, I will stop at nothing to get him off her. I roll the window of my Camry down and listen. It is eerily quiet. No arguing, no crashing plates, nothing to denote an argument.

The feeling that something is terribly wrong overwhelms me and I climb out of the car. My feet drag up the weed choked sidewalk and down the four steps to the basement door. I knock, my fist loud on the wood.

No sound comes from inside.

"Aubry? You here?" I call, too loud.

Still nothing.

The green paint on the door is cracked and I run a fingernail under one of the chips, not sure what to do. The chip falls away and lands on the toe of my black sneaker. Annoyed, I brush it away.

"Aubry?" I call with more desperation. "Brent?" I cup my face and press my nose against the glass of the small window in the front door. My breath fogs up the glass and I can't see in.

I pull my face away, wipe the glass and try again. The interior of the apartment is too dark to see anything beside the basic shapes of furniture. Next to the door is a smiling frog with a fake flowering plant in it. I know Aubry hides a key under the frog. I've told her how unsafe that is. It's the first place anyone would look for the key. As a reporter for the TV news, I've learned a few things.

Aubry, in her usual easy manner, brushed off my concerns. "If anyone really wanted to break in, they'd just smash a window," she'd said. "The key is for people like you, non-criminals who just need in."

I tip the smiling frog and retrieve the key, glad she didn't listen to me.

The key glides in easily, but there was no need for it. The door is unlocked.

A sick sense slides into my belly, the special sense I try desperately to avoid. The pizza I ate earlier flops sickeningly.

I push the door open onto the dark room.

The first thing I notice is the smell, the heavy, metal smell that I know instinctively is blood. I scream Aubry's name and scramble for the light switch. The room floods with light.

The body lies near the center of the room, in front of the couch, the legs spread across the colorful rug. Face-down, I only see the blond hair. Blond hair like mine, just not as long. I blink in shock, staring at the hair. One section is matted and red, a pool of blood spreading out from the head. Under the couch is a bat, red staining the business end of it.

The face is turned away from me. The black t-shirt and jeans could be worn by a man or woman. As the initial shock begins to fade, I realize the shoulders are too broad, the hair is long and blond, but not as long as Aubry's.

Brent wears his hair like that.

I drop to my knees near the body, but not too close. "Brent?" I whisper, knowing he won't be answering. With shaking fingers, I do the only thing that seems appropriate, feel for a pulse.

His neck is cold to the touch.

I snap my hand back.

The pizza flip flops in my stomach, rushes to be released.

I run for the front door and barely make it to the bushes before the pizza comes up. I drop to my knees as I vomit. My stomach empty, my mind is full of one thought.

"Where is Aubry?"

I climb onto shaky legs and go back into the apartment. I run from room to room, but Aubry is not here.

I close my eyes and focus, hoping to get some kind of idea about what happened here.

Nothing.

All I know is Brent is dead and Aubry is gone.

Desperate, I call her number again, begging her to answer.

A phone rings in the distance, outside. I follow the

sound and find her phone in the bushes, not far from where I lost my pizza.

My legs finally give out and I sink onto the steps leading down to her apartment. This doesn't look good for my sister. There can only be two stories here. She either killed Brent and took off without her phone or her car.

Or she's been taken and is in major trouble.

Aubry is not a murderer. Of that I'm sure.

But if Brent was coming after her, if he attacked her and she fought back?

I can't call the police. They will immediately think she did this. I look at her phone in the bushes and at her car parked on the curb.

If she was running from the cops, she'd have taken both.

I light another smoke and rack my brain for who can help. Only one person comes to mind. Someone that might be able to tell me what actually happened here.

The one person I dislike as much as I love my sister.

With tears threatening and my voice choking, I dial Gabby McAllister.

"I already told you, I don't want to be interviewed," she barks into the phone.

I swallow hard against the tears, "Gabby? I need your help."

"What's wrong?"

"My sister has disappeared and I'm afraid to call the cops. You have to help me find her."

Gabby hesitates, I'm sure wondering how desperate I must be to call her. "You do know I'm with both Lucas and Dustin right now."

I hadn't thought that far ahead. "You can't tell them," I snap. "At least not yet. Please, Gabby. This is my sister, we're talking about. I need help. You know I'm out of ideas if I'm calling you."

Another long moment of silence as Gabby thinks. "Where are you?" she finally asks.

My shoulders slump in relief as I give her the address. "You'll come alone?"

"For now. That's all I can promise."

Chapter 2

GABBY

My mouth hangs open in shock as I slide the phone back in my pocket. My entire family stands in Grandma Dot's kitchen, all eyes on me.

"Who was that?" Grandma asks with concern.

I fiddle with the necklace Lucas gave me for Christmas and say, "Lacey Aniston."

"That reporter lady that ambushed you the other day?" Mom asks.

I nod, my mind scrambling for a way to leave the dinner Grandma has planned without telling Lucas and Dustin where I'm going. Lacey doesn't want the cops involved. Maybe she shouldn't have called someone so closely involved with the only two detectives in River Bend, Indiana.

"Uh, I got to go." I direct the words to Grandma,

hoping she'll be the easiest to convince. "Lacey needs my help with something."

"Why would she ask you? I didn't get the feeling you two are friends," Mom pipes in, not helping at all.

"They're not." Lucas's voice is firm. "What's going on?"

I wrap the chain of my necklace around my finger then realize how nervous the act makes me look and drop it. "She just needs me. Please, its work. I can't tell you."

My brother, Dustin, makes a sound of disgust. "When we try to block you from our work you get all upset."

He's right, but I won't admit that now. Instead, I use him as a target to get me out of Grandma's kitchen without having to answer any more questions. "Crap on a cracker, Dustin, then you know what I'm talking about don't you? Can you give Lucas a ride home after dinner?"

"You're actually leaving for Lacey?" Lucas says. "That must have been some phone call." His hand is already digging his car keys out of his pocket to hand to me, trusting I know what I'm doing.

I love this man.

"I'll drive your handsome detective home if he needs a ride," Grandma says, breaking the tension in the room.

"First, eat a bit of something. You know how you get when you're hungry. Can't have you attacking Lacey because you skipped dinner." She hands me a roll and a piece of fried chicken. I drop a kiss on her thin cheek and whisper, "Thank you."

Lucas walks me out onto the porch. "You'll bring the car back tonight?" he asks suggestively.

I give him a kiss totally different than the one I gave Grandma. "Wouldn't miss it."

"Be careful, Gabby. I know Lacey asked for your help, but you two together makes me nervous. I wish you'd tell me what was going on."

"Honestly, I'm not completely sure." I take a bite out of the chicken leg Grandma gave me. "Wow, this is good. Wish I could stay."

Lucas looks about to say I can, but thinks better of it. He, of all people, should understand about being called out of family dinners to work.

I wave the chicken leg at him and climb into his car, secretly a little upset that Lacey called me and not the police. Although if she'd called the cops, it would be Lucas and Dustin's dinner that was ruined as well, not just mine.

I find Lacey sitting on a set of steps leading to what looks like a basement apartment in a large Victorian age home in the oldest part of town. The house is dark and looming, Lacey's unnaturally blond hair glows against the gloom.

My sneakers sound loud on the sidewalk as I make my way to her. Half way up the walk, I smell the smoke. I hadn't realized Lacey was a smoker. A drinker, sure, but not a smoker.

She hears me approach and looks over her shoulder so fast, her bright hair swirls around her. She must wear expensive mascara because, it's obvious in the pale light that she has been crying, but her makeup hasn't run down her face. Besides the red rims around her eyes and the pinkness of her running nose, she looks as beautifully made up as ever.

A surge of jealousy is quickly followed by a pang of self-consciousness. I run a hand over my wild curls and wish I had at least put on some lip gloss. I had applied a minimal amount of eyeliner before going to Grandma's, just enough to make me look like I tried, but that's it.

I chew on my bare lower lip nervously. I don't know

the last time Lacey and I have ever been alone together. She usually has a cameraman with her when she ambushes me. Or that time I saw her at the store, she was with a friend. I'm not sure how to act under these strange circumstances.

When Lacey sees me, she stubs out her cigarette and adds the butt to the small pile on the step next to her. She gives me a quick once over from unruly curls to scuffed sneakers, then jumps to her feet.

"Gabby, I'm so glad you came." She flies up the steps and throws her arms around me. I go stiff at the sudden embrace, terrified. If Lacey is shook up enough to actually touch me, to *hug* me, then things must be really bad.

I remove myself from her as delicately as possible. "I told you I would come," I say lamely, unsettled. "Why don't you tell me what's going on."

"My sister Aubry didn't show up for our regular Sunday night pizza dinner," she starts. I have trouble imagining Lacey with family and eating pizza. I have trouble picturing her as a human woman at all. "I got a, a feeling, that something was wrong, so I came here to her apartment." She motions to the door. "And I found him.

Brent. He's - ." She twists a long lock of her hair around her finger then lets it fall. "Aubry's not here, but her car and her phone are here." She twists the hair again, lets it fall, twists it again. The feverish motion is making me anxious. "I'm hoping you can, you know, do what you do, figure out what happened to Aubry, where she is."

At the moment, I'm more concerned with the mysterious Brent. I turn my back on the crazy hair twisting and hurry into the apartment. I find him on the floor of the living room, his blood pooled next to his head, seeping into the colorful rug.

"Lacey," I shout. "You didn't tell me you found a dead man. We have to call Lucas and Dustin."

"You promised, no cops. At least not yet. They will think Aubry did this to him and I know she didn't."

"But we can't just leave him here."

"We won't. He's not going to get any deader than he is. Please, take a look around, touch things or do whatever you need to. Nothing matters except finding Aubry." She has stopped twirling her hair and is staring me down with a determined expression I'm more familiar with on her face.

I take a step away from her, holding up my hands.

"Okay. I'll do what I can." I look around the room, the crime scene. "We shouldn't be in here, messing with things. Did you touch anything earlier?"

"No. Well, I mean, I tried to find a pulse on Brent, but he was cold."

"You didn't touch anything else?"

"I just looked around quick for Aubry."

"That's good." I scan the room, note the bat with blood on it under the couch. The murder weapon.

"Are you just going to stand there looking around or are you going to do something? My sister is in danger and you're wasting time."

I know what I need to do, but getting visions is a very personal and vulnerable thing, especially when a murder is involved. I loathe the idea of doing it in front of Lacey.

I stall, "Not to be indelicate, but you do know I don't do this for free, right?"

"For God's sake, Gabriella, Daddy will pay you anything you want, just get busy."

I lower my voice to a growl. "You call me Gabriella again and I'll walk out that door and call the police. Understand?"

Lacey takes a deep breath and blows it out. With an

effort of will, she says politely, "I understand. We will pay your fee. Now please, do something."

I'd hoped mentioning money would make her change her mind. I would give anything to be back at Grandma Dot's with my family, not kneeling before a murdered man about to see his death, witnessed by the person I dislike the most in the world. I pull off my left glove.

"God, please give me the strength to help her and not lose my cool," I pray silently. Out loud, I say. "Let me see what needs to be seen."

I touch Brent's cold hand and the vision jolts into me.

A woman's scream, Aubry are you okay? Running into the living room, the pressure in my head.

I don't feel Brent hit the floor. He was dead before he reached it.

When I come back to myself, Lacey is staring at me with something close to horror. I flick my eyes at her. "Is that what you do? That's all there is to it? You say a prayer and touch his hand?"

"What did you think I did?" I ask defensively.

She shrugs. "I don't know. Say some incantations, wave your arms around, something more interesting and dramatic."

I rock back on my heels, "Sorry to disappoint you. But that's it."

"So what did you see?"

"Not much. He heard Aubry scream and came out from the bedroom there. He was hit in the head and died instantly. Thank heavens he didn't suffer."

"Did you see who hit him? It wasn't Aubry, was it? I mean, of course it wasn't."

The bat is under the couch, a few inches of the handle sticking out. I really want to touch it, but I don't know how to do it without messing up the crime scene and leaving fingerprints.

Lacey sees me eyeing the bat. "Can you tell who swung the bat if you touch it?"

"Maybe," I hedge. "But I can't touch the murder weapon. The police might be able to pull prints off of it."

"I don't care about that. It could take forever to find a match and you could figure it out right now."

She has a point. A point I would make to Dustin if he were here. Lacey can sense me wavering.

"Maybe just touch it in a place where they won't be looking for prints, like half way up the bat."

I stare at the wooden play thing turned deadly weapon

and weigh the consequences. Dustin, and probably Lucas, will be upset that I'm here at all once they find out that poor Brent has been murdered. I could help the case along in just a few moments. They can fingerprint me and eliminate mine from any others on the bat.

Crouched on the balls of my feet, I gingerly reach for the bat, careful to touch it with just the tips of my fingers and to not move it.

A sick darkness inside. Surprise at Brent, determination to finish the job. Need her. Not you. Only need her. Not you. A sick enjoyment as the bat swings.

The vision knocks me on my rear. My head swirls with the repeated words.

"What did you see?" Lacey asks anxiously.

I climb to my feet and hang my head, my hands on my knees. "Give me a sec," I pant. The intensity in the killer's mind knocked the sense right out of me. Lacey shuffles uncomfortably, she raises a hand as if she's going to put it on my back to comfort me, but I shoot her a look and she drops it again.

"We need to call Lucas," I finally manage to say.

"Did you see who killed him?"

I shake my head vigorously, "No. But whoever he is,

he's nuts. He kept saying, 'need her.' I can only imagine he's talking about Aubry."

Lacey gasps and breaks into tears. "And now he has her."

I nod. "Maybe I can find something, anything else to help lead us to who took her." I begin scanning the room. "And I'm calling Lucas and Dustin." I pull the phone from my pocket as I walk into the kitchen and flip the light on.

The phone slips through my bare fingers and clatters to the faded linoleum. "Lacey, don't come in here."

Of course, she comes right away. "Oh my God," she exclaims. "I didn't turn the light on before, I was just looking for her and she wasn't in here."

Aubry isn't here, but she left blood behind, lots of it. It's spattered on the fridge, on the wall, on the clock with the hands in the shape of a spoon and a fork. Dried dark red, the blood is streaked, but luckily not pooled heavily.

I retrieve my phone from the floor and call Lucas.

Chapter 3

GABBY

Lacey takes the phone from my hand and deliberately hangs up on Lucas before it rings.

"Hey," I protest, snatching my phone back.

"If that's my sister's blood, I want to know. Go do your thing." Lacey's voice is cold, broking no argument.

The largest spatter is on the fridge, bright against the white of the door. As I approach, the motor inside kicks on. The noise is loud in the hush of the room, making me jump. I expect Lacey to laugh at me, but she is solemnly waiting.

I reach out my left hand and touch the bloody metal door.

The vision happens fast, a blur of sensations.

Shock, why are you here? Worry for Brent. White hot pain in the face and warm blood spraying. Hard hands on wrists, dragging, kicking.

As Aubry is removed from the vicinity of the blood, I lose her.

"You said you found her phone?"

Lacey nods and hands it to me, "It was in the bushes out front."

I don't lecture her on tampering with a crime scene, just take the phone, hoping for more clues. I haven't gotten a good look at whoever hit her and took her.

The phone is full of fear and panic, overriding conscious thought before it is knocked from Aubry's hand.

"I can't get anything from it. She wanted to call for help, but wasn't able."

Then Lacey does something completely unexpected. She puts her own hand on the phone, over mine. I feel a shimmer of something slide up my arm and my tattoo tingles. "Try again," she commands, closing her eyes and concentrating.

With Lacey's energy combined with mine, I get more.

Aubry sees Brent on the floor, a man with a bat standing over him. She takes the phone from her pocket to call for help, but is hit in the nose before she can use it. She's dragged out of the kitchen and through the front door. Terror screams through her as a rag is shoved in her mouth.

Lacey moans and her knees buckle.

I watch her fall to the floor in surprise.

"What did you just do?" I ask, flabbergasted, my mind not wanting to believe.

Lacey's hair hides her face and she refuses to look up. "You know what I did."

I swallow hard, no response forming on my confused tongue.

"If you tell anyone, I swear I will ruin you." I don't doubt the threat.

"I didn't know you had the gift?"

Lacey stands suddenly, shoves her face close to mine. "I do not. Don't even say the words. I just need to help my sister and I'll do whatever I can." She speaks so violently, little drops of spittle fly against my face.

She storms out of the living room and onto the steps, lighting a cigarette with shaking hands.

"There's nothing to be ashamed of," I try.

She swirls and faces me again. "I'm warning you, Gabby. Not another word." She takes a deep drag from the cigarette and blows it out slowly. "So we know a man took her. I didn't get a good look at his face, but that's the first time I've ever done anything like that. Did you see him?"

I shake my head. "Bad news is, he's not against using violence."

Lacey blows smoke again and makes a sound of disgust. "I suppose you have some good news?"

"Good news is, if he wanted her dead, he would have killed her here."

The sound Lacey makes is half way between a wail of pain and a laugh. "Some good news." She stubs out her smoke and lights another. "Is there anything else you can tell me? Anything else you can sense?"

I hold up my hand and really concentrate, listen to the wind, listen to my tattoo, pray for a miracle. A car wavers into view, a dark blue four door driving north. "He may have been in a dark blue car. Does that mean anything to you?"

Lacey thinks a moment. "No. Nothing. I mean I know people that drive dark blue cars but that doesn't really limit the suspect pool."

"Can you think of anyone that would want to hurt Aubry, or would want to take her from Brent. It seems the man Brent was just in the way. The killer seemed surprised to find him here. Does she have a crazy jealous ex?"

"She's been with Brent for over a year. They moved in here together a few months ago. The last man she dated was Justin Henna. He's a nice guy. I don't see him hitting anyone with a baseball bat. Besides, he broke up with her like two years ago. Last I heard he was with some new girl."

"Did the man we-," I swallow, "I saw in the vision look like Justin? I didn't get good look at him, but maybe -."

Lacey shakes her head. "Just impressions."

"I'm going to take another look around, and then I'm going to call Lucas," I tell her firmly. "We've gotten lucky that none of the other tenants of this house have come home yet, but they will. We need to get the scene secured and have Lucas and Dustin start looking for Aubry as soon as possible. Plus, there's Brent to deal with."

Lacey sniffles. "Poor Brent. He may not have been great for Aubry, but he didn't deserve this." Her hands shake as she takes another smoke from her pack although the one in her fingers is only half gone.

I gently take the pack away from her. "I think you've had enough cigarettes for a while." I nod towards the alarmingly large pile of butts on the step. "Just sit down and wait for the detectives. I think the shock is finally kicking in for you. Do you need anything?"

Lacey obeys and sinks to sit on the steps. "I need my sister back, and Brent to be alive."

Her pain tears at me. I barely recognize the broken woman huddled on the step. I need Lucas. He's used to dealing with family in this type of crisis. I'm not sure if I should sit with her and put my arm around her or what. I start to sit down, but she stops me.

"Get back in there and do whatever you can. Once the cops get here, they won't let you near the scene again, even I know that. You might find one tiny scrap of something that will lead to where he's taken Aubry."

She's desperate and grasping for a miracle, but I stand back up and think. I can't get more from Aubry, she was too scared to think clearly and leave me something to work with.

I get an idea and reach for the inside door handle. I avoid door handles as a rule, especially old ones like in this house. The kidnapper had to touch this handle to get

Aubry out.

He's going to be so pleased we got you. Pride, excitement.

That's all I see.

"Crap on a cracker," I exclaim as I let go of the handle. "He said 'we got you'. There's two of them."

Too late, I realize that I just left my fingerprints where the kidnapper's prints are.

Dustin is going to lose his temper at my stupid mistake.

Chapter 4

DUSTIN

I watch Gabby tell Lucas good-bye on Grandma Dot's back porch with trepidation. Lacey Aniston and Gabby have been at each other's throats since High School. I can't imagine a scenario in which Gabby would willingly leave to help her.

Lucas watches his car drive away with Gabby in it then feels me staring at him out the window. He shrugs, attempting unconcern. I know my partner and my best friend too well to fall for it.

"Want to go follow her?" I ask as he re-enters the kitchen.

My question gets me a smack with a hot pad from Grandma. "You leave your sister to her business. If she has to work, she has to work. Not like you haven't been called out from dinners before."

Alexis makes a sound of derision, startling us all. I swing my eyes to my wife, who until now has sat quietly at the table, holding Walker. Her face burns red at making the sound out loud and drawing attention.

"A little help?" I ask Lucas, needing some male support.

Grandma shoves a heaping platter of baked chicken into his hands, stopping any remark he might have made. "Just eat. Emily and I didn't make all this food for nothing."

Mom brings a tray of macaroni and cheese. "Made from scratch, not a box," she says a she sits it on the table. The food looks so good, I let thoughts of Gabby and Lacey fade away and concentrate on dinner with my family.

After we eat, Lucas begins clearing the table and I join him. I'm happy to have something to keep my hands busy. Something is niggling at me. I keep checking the driveway, expecting to see Gabby returning in Lucas's car, even though she asked us to give him a ride home.

At the sink, I say quietly, "You don't think they'd actually fight?"

Lucas knows who I mean immediately and makes a

small sound of laughter. "For Lacey's sake, I sure hope not." I can tell by the pinched look around his eyes, he's worried, too.

"Did she say where she was meeting her?"

"She didn't tell me anything." We both gaze out the window above the sink, looking for her to pull in. The women talk quietly at the table. Walker babbles and answers their questions of 'what does a pig say'.

A perfect family moment.

Lucas's phone rings in his pocket.

I turn off the water I'm using to rinse the dishes and turn to Alexis, apology covering my face.

She stares at me with a mixture of concern and anger then looks away.

Lucas is saying, "We'll be right there," as I'm making my good-byes to Grandma and Mom. "Can one of you take Alexis and Walker home?"

Lucas has hung up and the question hangs in the quiet of the room.

"Is she okay?" Mom asks Lucas.

"She's okay, but we have to go."

"Is it bad?" Grandma asks.

I glance at Lucas for confirmation. He opens his mouth

then closes it again.

"I wonder how many other families have dinners like this where one by one the members mysteriously leave and can't say why?" Alexis's voice is choked, startling me.

"I'm sorry," I say uselessly.

"Just don't. I know the drill." The venom in her words surprises us all. Until recently, Alexis has been nothing but supportive. "Emily, can you please take Walker and I home now? Unless you important men can drop us off on your way to wherever it is you need to go." She darts her eyes to Lucas who shakes his head.

Alexis stands suddenly, gathering Walker against her. "Emily?"

"Of course," Mom stammers. "Anything you need."

Alexis makes a sound of disgust. "What I need? Right." She puts Walker on her hip, tosses his few toys into his bag then slings the bag over her shoulder.

The rest of us watch her in shock. Outward displays of emotion are not Alexis's way. I should say something, should soothe the situation.

I don't know the words. I look at my wife with a mixture of anger at the scene she's making and guilt that she's so upset. "I don't know what you want me to say," I try.

She looks away, and turns the handle of the kitchen door. "Grandma Dot, thank you for dinner. Sorry we all have to leave so suddenly." She chokes on the last words then takes Walker out onto the porch.

Mom is getting her shoes on and gathering her purse, embarrassed. She kisses my cheek and follows Alexis outside. Lucas, Grandma and I watch as Mom's new little white car drives away.

"Any idea what that was about?" I ask Grandma.

"How'd you feel when Gabby left?"

"This is different."

Grandma places a dish in the sink, "Not to her, it isn't." She wipes her hands on a dish towel. "Gabby's okay?"

"She's the one that called," Lucas says. "She's fine, but we really need to go."

I brace myself for a complaint from Grandma, but none comes. "Watch over that girl," Grandma says to Lucas. "And you play nice. I feel trouble coming and you two will need each other."

I don't like the premonition in her words. "I can't make any promises, but I'll try."

Lucas is anxious to get going and after a quick hug and

thank you, I follow him onto the porch.

"So?" I ask.

"Lacey's sister Aubry has been kidnapped and her boyfriend has been murdered." He says the words matter-of-factly, belying the weight of them.

"And Lacey called Gabby instead of us?"

"Let's just get there. If Aubry really has been kidnapped, then we've lost valuable time already."

Chapter 5

GABBY

Lacey and I sit quietly together on the front steps leading down to the basement apartment. She lights a smoke and offers me one. I shake my head.

"Right," she mumbles and takes a long drag. She doesn't aim her exhale at me, but she doesn't turn her head away either.

I fight the urge to cough at the smoke, not wanting to give her the satisfaction.

"What will happen when they get here?" she asks after several minutes. "I've reported at crime scenes, of course, but only after the fact."

"The first thing they'll do is make us leave, if I know my brother."

Lacey makes a sound that might have been a bark of laughter. "Dustin is sure a piece of work. He never has a comment for me, barely tolerates it when I show up."

I don't know how to respond. Its one thing for me to be annoyed by him, quite another to have Lacey Aniston running her mouth about him.

"He has a job to do," I finally say.

"So do I. The least the police could do is give us the information we seek."

"Will you report on this?" I ask. "It's different when it's your own name in the news." I'm thinking of all the times Lacey has dragged my name through the mud on her broadcasts.

Lacey begins twirling her hair nervously. "I don't know. If it will help find Aubry." She looks over her shoulder anxiously. "Where are they, already? We're wasting time just sitting here."

I rub my tattooed left forearm, run my fingers along the lines of the delicate cross. It's a nervous habit that Lacey picks up on.

"Nice tattoo," she says, almost sounding impressed. "I didn't take you for the religious type."

I laugh out loud at that. If she only knew.

"Do you have any?" I say these words instead of the smart retort that popped into my mind.

"Just a butterfly on my hip. Aubry and I got them on a

trip to Mexico a few years ago. Different butterflies, but in the same place." Lacey pulls the top of her pants down a few inches to show me. The butterfly is beautiful, but the incident feels bizarre. A few hours ago, Lacey was my enemy, now she's showing me her hip. "Aubry's has more green and blue instead of orange and yellow."

She covers the tattoo and looks towards the street. "Seriously, where are they?" Her hands shake as she takes another drag from her cigarette. This time she exhales away from me.

"They were at Grandma Dot's. They should be here any minute." I stand and pace the four steps across the patio. "Speaking of family, we need to call your parents."

"Can't." She runs a hand through the ends of her perfectly blond hair. "They're on a Mediterranean cruise. A 'see all the wonders of the ancient world without leaving the ship' kind of thing. They are supposed to be home tomorrow morning, though."

"Crap on a cracker. They need to know what's going on."

"Spotty cell service out on the water, but I can try." She takes out her phone and dials. After a moment, she says, "Straight to voicemail. I'm not leaving a message about something like this."

"Lucas will figure out how to get ahold of them."

Her eyes search my face, tears starting to well. "That makes it seem so real. She's really missing." I continue to pace, her agitation adding to mine. She suddenly grabs my wrist. "You have to find her," she begs. "What if the police think she killed Brent and took off? They won't look for her like you will."

Her palm is damp and hot, her grip on my left wrist tight. My tattoo tingles when she touches me. I listen with half my mind for the words that usually follow a tattoo tingle. Words from God. The other half of my mind, the petty half, is listening to Lacey beg. A tiny part of me, a part I'm not proud of, is enjoying seeing her perfect facade cracked a bit.

"What do you want me to do that I haven't already done?"

"I don't know." Her voice rises and she scans the street again. "Just go in and look around again before they get here. Maybe we missed something the first time."

I'd been aching to go back into the apartment and snoop around this whole time. I was trying to follow protocol, trying to not do something to tick off Dustin.

She grabs my wrist again and this time the tingle is stronger and the words I only half listened for before speak loud and clear.

Go in again.

"Quick," I drag Lacey to the front door. "The boys will not be pleased if they find us in here again."

Touching as little as possible, I open the front door and let us in.

This time, I smell the blood, mixed with the lovely scent of vanilla coming from a candle still burning on a side table. The tiny flame and homey scent feel way out of place at a crime scene.

Before I can stop her, Lacey blows the candle out. "Fire hazard," she says enigmatically. "Aubry loved vanilla."

"She still does." I say gently.

We stand side by side and stare at the blood on the kitchen wall and floor. "You really think she is okay, even with all this blood?"

"I've seen more, and he turned out to be okay." I touch the scar on my eyebrow. I hadn't meant to mention the night my father was "murdered" and I was hit on the head getting the injury that brought forth my psychic gift.

Lacey darts her eyes at me. "My offer for an exclusive interview about that whole story still stands. The publicity could be great for your shop."

Hounding me for an interview is more like the Lacey I'm used to. "Let's discuss that type of thing later," I say gently. "What else can we do before we're kicked out of here?"

"Did you want to try touching, the, you know." She points to the small puddles on the floor.

"Maybe if we do it together." I have my gloves off and grip Lacey's bare hand before she can respond. I pull her down until we are both kneeling by a puddle.

I touch the blood with one fingertip of my left hand. I feel Lacey stiffen, her grip growing tight.

"Just relax into it. Don't try to block the energy. Open your mind to it."

Her grip releases some of its steel and her breathing slows to a normal pace.

Now that Lacey is centered, I open my own mind. "God, let me see what you need me to see."

The vision comes just like before. Lacey goes stiff again as we live through Aubry's surprise and pain as she gets hit. It's the same vision I already had, this time a little more clear, the emotions a little more raw. Lacey lets out a whimper when Aubry is smashed in the nose and the blood sprays around the kitchen.

She claws at my fingers, trying to break the contact. She has both hands on my right, my left is still touching the blood.

The vision shifts from Aubry's thoughts and feelings to something shadowy, shifting. I'm distracted by Lacey pulling at my hand, feel my grip slipping.

The surrounding mist whispers, "All are one."

The vision is broken when long nails dig into my hand. "Let go!" Lacey shouts. "I don't want to see."

I release her wrist and my head clears. "Did you hear that?" I gasp.

"All I heard was my sister's terror. Why did you make me do that? It's bad enough knowing something bad happened, I don't need to live through it, too."

The last thing I saw, the words "All are one," replays in my mind so strongly I have trouble remembering what Lacey is talking about.

"You didn't hear it? Did you see the mist?"

She's saved from answering by a bellow from the front door. "What in the world are you two doing in here?" I don't know the voice well, but the authoritative manner I remember clearly.

My head sinks and I whisper to my lap, "Crap on a cracker." I then shove to my feet and turn to face Chief Simmons.

Chapter 6

GABBY

Followed on the heels of Chief Simmons's unpleased welcome another familiar voice pipes in.

"Oh, heck no, you can't be in here," Coroner Gomez exclaims. "The press and the psychic? Simmons, what is wrong with your department?"

Lacey and I stand side by side. Aubry's blood stains the tip of my finger. I slide my gloves back on as quickly as possible. Gomez still sees the blood.

"You touched the blood?" Her voice drips with disgust.

Anything I can say will not fully explain what we were doing, at least not to these two.

"Sorry," I say lamely.

"Gabby, just get out." Simmons rubs his face in exasperation. "You, too, Lacey. And don't even think about reporting on what you've seen here."

Lacey straightens her back. "I'm not leaving. This is my sister's blood. She's in trouble and you need to find her."

Chief Simmons seems surprised by this information. "Aubry is missing? This is her place?"

Lacey nods sadly. "And that's her boyfriend over there. I found him when I came to check on Aubry. She didn't show up for Sunday night pizza."

Gomez is already kneeling near Brent's body. "You didn't touch anything in here, did you? Didn't try any of your hocus pocus stuff?"

I swallow hard. I have to tell the truth or compromise the scene and the case even further.

"I touched the bat, and Aubry's phone, and the door handle. That's it. We really were trying to be careful and respectful."

"That blood on your finger is careful and respectful?" she retorts, tossing her long french braid over her shoulder in agitation. Normally, Gomez bothers me. Tonight, I'm bothered by how correct she is. I really screwed this up.

"Just take my prints and my DNA and you can rule me out of anything."

"Take mine, too," Lacey pipes in. "We are really sorry,

Coroner Gomez." She beams at the woman. The submissive tone is one I've never heard Lacey use. I imagine it serves her well on getting people to talk to her on her stories. She's only ever bullied me.

Gomez seems mollified by the tactic. She motions to a tech that just entered the house and gives him directions to take our samples.

"Then get out of here," she says.

"Wait outside, she means." Simmons says. "We'll still need your statements once McAllister and Hartley get here to take them." The smallest note of annoyance echoes in his voice.

"We're here. We're here. Glad to know we were missed." The man I love enters the room. Despite the situation and the barely veiled glare he sends my way, I'm pleased to see him.

"Gabby, Lacey. I think Chief said something about waiting outside," Lucas says charmingly.

I follow him to the door, with Lacey close behind. Night has fallen in earnest now and the light bars on the cruisers that have just pulled up dance in red and blue streaks across the front of the Victorian house turned apartment building.

Lucas waits until we are on the front walk before starting in on us. "I thought you said you would wait outside?" He says quietly, hooking a thumb in his belt.

I see Dustin approaching and feel irritation rising in my belly.

"We were trying to help." I explain. "Once you got here, we knew we couldn't be in there. I wanted to see what we could see before then."

"Let me guess," Dustin says with heavy sarcasm once he joins our group. "She wanted to touch things first."

I raise my chin, "Good thing I did. Aubry has been kidnapped. I know it looks like a lover's spat gone bad in there, but it isn't. Someone hit Brent and then attacked and kidnapped Aubry. Two people actually. I think."

The men look at each other. I've seen this same exchange before. I think of it as their "we're gonna believe her in the end, we might as well now" look. Lucas caves first.

"You didn't tell that to the chief or to Gomez, did you?"

"No." I look away. "She was more interested in finding out I touched the murder weapon and a few other things."

"Gabby! Is this your first day on a crime scene?"

54

Dustin exclaims. "That's rule one. Touch nothing."

I stare at my shuffling feet. "I know. I just had to see." Lacey has watched the whole family scene in silence.

"I asked her to do it," she comes to my defense, surprising us all. "I begged her to help me. If she could see something that will lead to finding my sister, I'm willing to take the chance."

Lucas flips open a notebook from a back pocket. He's still wearing the clothes he wore to Grandma Dot's. I wonder where the notebook came from. Does he keep them stashed in the car? Does he always have one with him and I just hadn't noticed. I stare at the notebook, asking him where it came from on the tip of my tongue.

"Tell me again exactly what you saw," he says.

I tell him how Brent heard a scream, got hit and was gone. "The killer mostly just said, 'need her'. It was creepy. He definitely came for Aubry. There's more than one person involved. I heard 'he's going to be so pleased we got you.'" I scan my memory for any more details that might help. I leave out the mist that said, 'All are one'. "A dark blue car, too. I think I saw that."

I can tell by Dustin's body language he'd rather be inside where the action was than out here listening to my visions. He shifts his weight from the ball of one foot to the other.

"We'll see if that matches with the evidence," Dustin says. A few quick strides and he's going down the steps to the basement apartment. "Hartley, you coming?" he tosses over his shoulder.

I rankle at being summarily dismissed. Lucas looks at me sheepishly. "He's in a bit of a mood," he tries to apologize.

"I know how my brother gets. It's fine." I yearn to take his hand or to touch his face. Any signal that he's not too mad at me. With Lacey standing next to me and the whole front yard now crawling with uniforms, this isn't the place for public displays of affection.

I console myself with staring at his handsome blue eyes. A flash of emotion passes between us.

"Jeez, get a room, you two," Lacey says and steps away.

"You know I'm going to get in trouble for you being inside. The chief is going to want to take it out on someone."

"I'm sorry," I say as contritely as possible. My hand raises to grasp his, but I catch myself just in time and lower it.

"Hartley, if you'd like to join us that would be much appreciated," Chief Simmons calls from the front door. "I mean if it isn't interfering with your date."

My cheeks blaze and Lucas backs away with a sheepish shrug. "Lacey, someone will be coming for your complete statement." To me, he says, "We'll contact you if we need anything else."

I understand the need for the professional detachment, but it rankles just the same. He softens it by a barely visible flutter of his fingers as a wave good-bye. He disappears into the hive of activity that the apartment has become.

"Looks like I've been dismissed," I say to Lacey. "Will you be okay?"

Her eyes are wet and she sniffles a little, but she nods. "Yeah. I'll be okay. I'm just glad they are doing something. It feels like forever since I realized she was gone."

I check the clock on my phone. "It's only been just over an hour since you called me. She can't be too far away yet."

"Why would someone take her? Aubry is the sweetest,

kindest girl. Who could want to hurt her?"

"We'll find her. Do you have anything of hers that I could take with me? Maybe I can try to get a connection."

Lacey slowly slides Aubry's phone out of her pocket.

"I can't take that. It's evidence."

"Please. If you can get something off it, take it. I can always turn it in tomorrow and say I forgot it was in my pocket."

I'm anxious to take the phone, but also know it's not quite the right thing to do. I stare at the dark rectangle in Lacey's palm for a moment, then grab the phone. In a moment, I've hidden it in my own pocket.

"Only until tomorrow," I say hurriedly. "I'll let you know if I get anything."

With the contraband phone pressing against my hip, I'm anxious to get out of here. With a last awkward pat on Lacey's shoulder, I turn to leave.

"Gabby McAllister?" a young man in a tech suit calls. "We need those samples before you go."

I'd forgotten my promise to give my DNA and prints. As I let the tech scrub the inside of my cheek with a q-tip, I can only think of the phone in my pocket and if it might actually let me see Aubry. I've never tried anything like it before and I'm anxious to get home where I can try in privacy.

The tech finishes getting my samples and moves on to Lacey's. "I'll call you as soon as I know anything. I can't promise anything, though," I tell her.

Lacey waits until the q-tip is removed from her mouth to respond. "Just do what you can. I don't have much hope it will work. I'm not expecting much from you."

After all we've been through together tonight, I expected a warmer send off than that. Lacey is once again twirling her hair. She smiles brightly at the young tech. This is the Lacey I've always known. I roll my eyes. Even in crisis, she can't help herself.

Chapter 7

GABBY

I sit on my bed, leaning against the wooden plank headboard. I stroke my cat, Chester's, gray head with my left hand and stare at the phone in my right. I wear thick gloves to protect me from the energy in the last thing Aubry touched before she was dragged away.

I feel guilty about the phone. Feel disloyal to Lucas and Dustin. If I had explained what I wanted to do, how any information I could get off of it would help the case, they may have let me. Probably would have allowed me to touch it again after I pressed the issue.

Instead, I stole evidence.

"Stop stalling and do something then," I snap out loud.

I sit up straight, my back stiff and determined. Chester

jumps away, startled by my sudden outburst.

I take one deep breath and decide I'm centered enough. Then I pull both gloves off and cradle the phone in my hands.

"Lord, let me see her. Let me find her."

The phone tingles a little, a thousand pricks of energy against my skin. In my mind, I feel the connection to her fingerprints, a tiny connection, but thousands of them.

I breathe deep again and focus on the pinpricks.

My wrists burn against narrow ropes. My mouth is dry against a wad of thin fabric. My nose is stuffy and only one nostril is clear. I panic I might suffocate and I sniff hard to clear it. Air flows and relief floods my adrenaline laden blood. I open my eyes, but see only the blindfold. A dim glow of orange seeps through the weave of the fabric, filling my sights but offering no clues. In the distance, dogs bark. Many dogs. I sit on something cushioned, but worn and poking into my rear, a sofa or a large chair. My hands are bound behind me.

The quiet squeak of a door opening focuses all my attention. Nearly silent footsteps cross the room, growing closer. Something brushes against my cheek.

"So lovely. Makes this more fun," a man says. His

voice is smooth, controlled.

My stomach roils with terror. For a moment I fear I will vomit against the fabric shoved in my mouth, then suffocate.

"Are you ready?" the voice asks. He must want me to reply, because he slowly pulls the fabric from my mouth. I gasp once, sucking in a lung full.

Then I scream.

Then I scream. My eyes fly open and I see the phone in my hands. The dark rectangle is still tingling and I throw it across the room. It hits the wall and bounces onto a pile of laundry.

Scrambling, I search for gloves, any gloves. I find one of the thick ones tangled in the blankets of my bed and slide it onto my left hand. My breath comes easier as I focus on searching for the other glove instead of thinking about the vision. I don't find the thick one, but I find a different glove at the foot of the bed. Once both hands are covered I begin to feel safe again.

I stare at the phone lying on top of the t-shirt and sweat pants I was planning on sleeping in tonight. They now seem tainted by the phone's presence.

Chester suddenly jumps on my lap, and I break out into

a nervous laugh. "As if I needed anything else to scare me right now," I say to the cat. He just rubs his head against my gloved hand, begging for attention. The familiar act calms my raw nerves. After a few moments, I feel steady again, ready to do what I know must be done, even if I get in trouble.

I pull the pillow case off my pillow and, using it as a sack, I scoop the phone inside, dirty t-shirt and all. I have no interest in seeing the rest of what happened or is happening to Aubry right now. I only want to save her.

To do so I need to tell what I saw and how I saw it.

Holding the bag away from my body, I climb into my Charger, leaving Lucas's car in my driveway. I toss the pillow case onto the passenger seat and search the center console for a stray caramel or piece of candy.

I find a caramel and pop it into my mouth. There's not much sugar in one candy, but after that wallop of a vision, I feel drained and thirsty. At a red light, I reach to the back floor boards and feel around for a can of soda. I often bring a Dr. Pepper with me when I go out. Sometimes I forget about them and they roll around the back until times like now.

My fingers close around an unopened can. When I

open the can, it fizzes out the hole and dribbles all down the front of my shirt.

"Crap on a cracker!" I swipe at the mess with a stray napkin. A car behind me honks and I realize the light has turned green. I pull forward and sip the bubbling soda. The fizzy mouthful isn't enough to quench my thirst and I drink heavily.

Even then, my mouth feels dry.

Thin fabric shoved against my tongue.

I'm either remembering the earlier vision, or feeling Aubry again, but the dryness of my tongue is hers.

Scared, I rub my tongue across the top of my mouth, trying to get rid of the sensation. "What's happening?" I ask the empty car.

My tattoo tingles and my head spins a bit. I take another drink of the Dr. Pepper, swishing it around before I swallow.

This does the trick and my tongue feels like mine again as I park down the street from Aubry's apartment. Official vehicles clog the street and crime tape flutters. Tears burn my eyes for Brent and for Aubry.

"Lord, please look after their loved ones," I say a quick prayer. "And help us find Aubry quickly."

I pick the pillow case up by the very edge of the fabric. After downing the rest of the Dr. Pepper, I climb out of the car, ready to face whatever I must to get the information I saw to Lucas and Dustin.

As I walk down the sidewalk, careful to keep the pillow case far from my bare knees, I search the faces of the patrolmen on duty. By a stroke of luck, I see Officer Patterson near the tape. He's looking across the street, not in my direction.

The yellow tape flutters and blue and red lights dance across it. I hope Patterson will keep looking the other way and I can sneak into the scene. I duck my head under the tape and take two steps inside before I hear my name.

"Gabby McAllister, what are you doing here?" Patterson asks. He seems more curious than upset. Maybe he doesn't know I was sent away.

"I was called in to, uh, do what I do," I lie.

Patterson steps back and lets me pass. "Right. Of course." He has been with me on cases before and knows exactly what I do and how I do it. He's one of the few people that accept me for who I am. I feel bad for lying to him. The guilt wins.

"Actually, I was already here," I tell him. "But I need

to talk to Lucas and Dustin right way."

Patterson's face clouds. "If you're not supposed to be here, maybe you should go."

I hold up the pillow case. "I have to get this back to them."

"A pillow?"

My face burns with guilt. "It's Aubry's cell phone."

"You can't have that," he says in a loud whisper. "Gomez was barking about it a little bit ago. Had us all looking for it in the bushes and everything."

"I know, I know. I brought it back."

Patterson steps out of my way. "Good luck," he says and lets me pass.

My feet want to drag as I approach the patio. I force them to keep moving and go down the few steps. The front door is open and a flurry of activity is buzzing inside. I duck my head in, holding the pillow case behind me.

I see Lucas down the short hall to the kitchen. He's talking to one of the crime scene techs. The overhead light glints off his dark hair. I watch him talk, drink him in a moment before I make him mad at me.

"What's she doing here again?" Coroner Gomez barks.

Every head in the room looks towards the door wearing expressions ranging from curiosity on those that don't know me well, to the black cloud of anger from Gomez and Chief Simmons.

I dare a glance at Lucas whose own face looks angry. "Can I talk to you?" I say as politely as possible. Dustin steps into view.

"Oh, Gabby," he says under his breath, but I can read his lips.

I feel my face burn, but I have to push on. I hold the bag out in front of me. "I have the phone. And some information you need."

"Simmons," Gomez shouts striding towards me with quick steps. "What kind of crime scene are you running here? This woman is a menace." She grabs the pillow case from me and reaches in. She holds up my dirty t-shirt. "Is this a joke?"

My entire body burns with shame and I'm conscious of everyone staring at me. "It's in there."

"Hartley," Simmons barks. "Get her outside."

Lucas takes me by the elbow and steers me back up the steps. "You've pushed it too far this time," he whispers near my ear. I knew he'd be mad, he has every right, but the venom still stings.

Dustin, Gomez and Simmons follow us onto the lawn. Patterson catches my eye then quickly looks away. I spot Lacey leaning against a cruiser nearby, her hair dancing with red and blue. She watches with open curiosity.

Once in the yard, Lucas drops my elbow and stands next to Dustin along with Gomez and Simmons. The combined glares nearly take my breath away.

"I know I shouldn't have taken the phone, but I wanted to see if I could contact Aubry. The phone is all I had."

Gomez rolls her eyes hard. "Contact her? Are you crazy?" She looks at Dustin and then Lucas. "She's crazy, right?"

I let the 'crazy' comment go. "I saw where she is. What's happening to her. She's tied up in a room somewhere."

"Oh, that's a big help," Gomez says sarcastically. "She's in a room somewhere. Now we know exactly where she is."

Once she says it out loud, I realize how unhelpful my information really is. I thought I had a good lead, really I have nothing. I feel worse than before.

"There's a man with her," I add.

Simmons and Gomez shake their heads in disgust.

"At least you know she didn't do that to Brent. You know you're dealing with a kidnapping," Lacey suddenly says behind me.

"We don't know anything," Gomez says. "The most likely scenario is the same story it usually is. She and the boyfriend got in a fight and she lost control. Then she ran. Happens all the time."

I look at Lacey whose mouth is open in horror.

"My sister did not do this. She's in trouble."

"She truly is. I saw it," I add.

"Even if that were true," Gomez retorts, with a toss of her long braid. "All you've done is waste our time and possibly messed up evidence. This phone is now covered in your prints and DNA." She looks over her shoulder and barks to a nearby tech. "Put a rush on the DNA tests for these two. I want their profiles ASAP so we can process this scene correctly. Legally." She steps close. She's so short, she barely reaches my chin, but she makes me shake just the same. "This is your last warning, Gabby," she hisses. "You mess with this case again, I will have you arrested. I should do it now, but we have this case to deal with and you've wasted enough time and resources."

She turns on her heel and stalks away.

Simmons says, "Hartley, get her statement and get her out of here. Then both of you get back to work. If she's right, Aubry Aniston is in trouble and we need to get to her as soon as we can."

I watch the Chief's retreating back in surprise. He believed my vision.

Lucas and Dustin exchange a look and shake their heads. "You are the luckiest person I've ever met," Dustin says. "If you weren't my sister, I'd arrest you for tampering."

"Thank you for not," I say genuinely. "I really am just trying to help."

"You're always trying to help. That's the problem," Lucas says. I'm shocked by the disgust still in his voice.

"You're mad at me?" The words pop out of my mouth.

"Of course I am. What you do reflects on both of us." He tosses his hands and says to Dustin. "You take her statement. I'm going back inside."

He storms away and a part of me tears inside. "Lucas?"

He keeps walking.

Dustin sighs heavily and takes out his notebook. I'm conscious of Lacey listening as he says, "Let's get this over with."

Chapter 8

LACEY ANISTON

I listen as Gabby gives her official statement to her brother. To his credit, he keeps his anger in check, just barely.

She finishes up with her version of events and Dustin snaps his book closed.

"Now go home," he says without preamble.

Gabby lifts her chin. "I said I would go. If you need anything."

Dustin glares at her, "We won't."

She looks towards the door of Aubry's apartment, no doubt looking for her boyfriend. I can't help feel bad for her a little. It's my fault she's in this mess.

Dustin looks at me, "You can go, too. We'll contact you when we have something."

"I don't want to go. I want my sister back," I protest.

"The best thing you can do is go home and wait. Let us handle this. We will contact your parents." Dustin checks his book. "You don't have any other info other than the cruise line they're on?"

"They are due back tomorrow morning. I tried calling, but keep getting voice mail."

"Hopefully we have Aubry back safe before they even know she's gone." I'm surprised at his soft tone.

"So you don't think she is guilty?"

He darts his eyes at Gabby. "No, I don't."

Gabby smiles widely. "Thank you."

"Don't get too cocky. We still don't have much to go on. Is there any other details you remember from what you saw?"

Gabby scrunches her face. "Dogs. I heard dogs barking."

Dustin seems unimpressed with this information. "Dogs, a room and a guy that's holding her. That's not much to go on."

Gabby shrugs. "It's something."

Dustin looks over my shoulder at a couple attempting to get under the crime tape. "Looks like the other tenants have come home. You two go now." With that, he walks to the confused couple at the tape.

I look toward Gabby. "Looks like we've been dismissed."

"Yeah. That happens a lot. Are you going home to wait?"

"No. I'm going to go get a crew and get this story on the air. A story might bring in a lead." I'm itching to get to work now. Needing to do something.

Gabby fiddles with her gloves, not wanting to leave, but unable to stay. "What are you going to do?"

"Probably go home like I've been told. Unless there's something you need me to do?" She sounds so hopeful.

"If you get anymore visions, please let me know. I know Dustin and Lucas will do their best, but everyone knows you have a special way to do things."

She nibbles her lower lip a moment. "You do, too, don't you?" She finally asks.

The camaraderie we've felt vanishes.

"That never happened." I narrow my eyes so she gets the point.

Her eyes widen, "Of course. Your secret is safe with me." She tosses her curls and turns to leave with another longing look at the door to the apartment.

I watch her duck under the tape and wonder what it must be like to be her. To have the gift and be so open about it. To not have to hide that part of herself.

A sudden rush of tenderness flows through me for the woman. She did come help me when I asked.

Alone on the front yard, surrounded by uniforms and yellow tape, the lights of the cruisers dancing in bright colors, I suddenly feel alone. I think of my son far away at with his father. I fish out a cigarette with shaking fingers and take a deep drag. The smoke does nothing to fill the void. I wish my parents were home already. I desperately wish Aubry would walk out the door, giving me crap for all the hassle.

I finish my smoke and stub it out. I open my empty hands to the night sky, tip my head back and stare at the stars.

What was it Gabby said just before she got her vision? "Lord, let me see what I need to see." I say the words over and over and open myself to the universe.

I listen with more than my ears, look with more than my eyes. "Aubry, where are you?"

A room flickers in candlelight, faded and peeling wallpaper covers a wall. Dogs bark in the distance.

A dog barks next door to Aubry's, breaking the tenuous connection.

"Lacey, are you okay?" Dustin is staring at me a few feet away. "You looked a little spaced out, there for a minute."

I run a hand through my hair and take a deep breath. My knees feel weak, but I'm not about to tell Dustin that.

"I'm fine. Just thinking about Aubry."

"Probably best you leave," he says, taking my elbow and gently leading me to the tape. "I promise we'll call as soon as we know anything new." He lifts the tape and I duck under.

It snaps back into place behind me. I know I won't be able to cross it again.

I debate telling him what I saw, but don't know how to explain it. Peeling wallpaper doesn't narrow the search much. It's not enough to expose my secret.

Dustin leaves me on the far side of the tape and goes back to work. I have work to do, too.

I pull out my phone and call into the TV station to tell them I have a story. My mind starts ticking through what I'll say on camera, what angle I'll use that might bring Aubry home.

Thankful to have work to do, something to keep me busy, I pace the tape and wait for my cameraman.

This story will get the most coverage of any story I've ever done. Whoever is holding Aubry better watch their back because I'm coming for them.

Chapter 9

GABBY

I feel Lacey watching me leave. I wish it was Lucas watching. I check over my shoulder, hoping to catch a glimpse of him. Hoping to see his crooked smile that will let me know we're okay.

I get the feeling we are not.

I may have pushed it too far tonight.

The truth is I would do it all again if it helps find Aubry.

My Charger roars into life and I leave the colorful crime scene behind. I had expected to sleep at Lucas's tonight, the way I have most nights lately.

Somehow, I don't think he wants to see me.

If he even gets to go home tonight.

I start towards home, but the car seems to have other plans. I soon find myself in Grandma Dot's driveway. The flicker of the TV tells me she's still up.

I let myself in the back door and Jet, her tiny black dog meets me with a wagging tail. I bend to scrub behind his ears saying, "Some guard dog you are."

He wriggles at my touch and runs to the front room.

"Is that you, Gabriella?" Grandma calls.

I find her in her recliner, crocheting a navy blue and cream afghan. Even when she's resting, she's working.

I flop down on the couch. "I'm surprised you're still up."

"I was waiting for you."

Jet jumps on my lap. "How'd you know I'd come? I didn't even know."

"If it wasn't tonight, it would have been in the morning. I was going to watch the news anyway and find out what's going on."

I pet Jet, not sure what I should tell her. If I know Lacey, it will be all over the news in a little bit anyway.

"Lacey's sister is missing and her boyfriend has been murdered."

"Aubry? Who'd take such a sweet girl?" Grandma's fingers freeze in surprise then start in on the crochet needle again.

"Multiple someones, I think. She's being held in a room somewhere with a guy. But I think he had help taking her from the house."

Grandma nods, not needing to ask how I know these things. "What does Dustin and Lucas think?"

"I'm pretty sure they are on my side, but the coroner is not a fan. She's running under the assumption that Aubry killed Brent and then took off. Without her phone or her car, and regardless of what Lacey and I saw."

Her fingers freeze again and she meets my gaze. "Lacey saw?"

I look down at Jet, angry I let that slip. I've never kept a secret from Grandma before, but this isn't my secret to keep.

I'm saved from having to answer by Lacey's face appearing on the TV. "This just in,"

Lacey tells the camera about her sister's disappearance. I brace myself for her to mention my part in the events, maybe even mention how I was kicked off the scene. She luckily leaves me out of it.

"Oh, dear," Grandma says when Lacey ends the story with a heartfelt plea for information. "That poor family. Anthony and Jenna must be going crazy with worry."

"They don't know yet. They are on their way home from a cruise. No one's been able to get ahold of them."

"I forgot they were gone on that." Little happens in this town that doesn't get discussed in the beauty shop chairs. "Mrs. Mott said they did the Mediterranean."

I stretch out my legs and lean back on the couch, exhausted from all the visions and the excitement of the night. "That's what Lacey said," I mumble.

Grandma turns off the TV and the room is mellow and comforting, lit only by a small lamp on a side table.

"Are you sleeping here?" she asks.

I curl onto my side, the couch sucking me into oblivion. "Just for a minute," I say as I kick off my shoes.

Grandma pulls a quilt from the back of the couch and tucks me in. "Get some rest. You're going to be going through a lot in the next few days with finding Aubry."

"I was kicked off the case," I point out through a yawn.

"When did that ever stop you?" she kisses my cheek and turns out the light.

I wake to Jet licking my face. It takes a few minutes to get my bearings. Beyond the living room curtains, the sun is just beginning to lighten the sky. I push Jet away from my nose and sit up.

I check my phone to see if I missed a call from Lucas or even from Lacey. There are no notifications.

Stretching my stiff neck, I follow the smell of coffee to the kitchen. Grandma is putting butter on toast.

"You hungry?"

"Always," I say and make myself some coffee heavy with vanilla creamer and sugar. Grandma hands me the toast. "I figured you wanted to get an early start this morning. I'm sure Lucas and Dustin could use a fresh pair of eyes. I doubt they got any sleep last night."

"I don't think I'm the eyes they want. I don't know what I can do." I bite into my toast.

"I'm sure you'll figure it out." Grandma brushes my concerns away.

I check my phone again, but it's still blank.

"He's not going to call while he's working," Grandma says. "You'll have to get in another way. She's the one that got you involved in the first place."

I chew toast, thinking. "I could offer my services to her parents," I say.

"There you go. Anthony has been a fan of yours." Grandma's known Anthony Aniston for years. He gets his hair cut here. "I'm sure he'll love any help he can get." She pours coffee into a thermos cup.

The sun is just starting to pink the sky. "You think he's back yet?"

She dollops the coffee with plenty of creamer and puts the lid on it. "One way to find out," she says and hands me the cup.

"You kicking me out?" I ask, amused.

"You have a young woman to find. The police have had all night to do it their way. You do it yours."

"Not sure what my way is," I say.

Grandma points to my arm, my cross tattoo.

"He knows."

I place my hand over my tattoo, Grandma adds her hand to mine. "Lord, guide Gabriella today. Lead her where you need her to go. Put a hedge of protection over Aubry and bless Brent's family and help them find peace in their loss."

"Let me see what I need to see," I add and say Amen.

As I let myself out the back door into the pink and orange sunrise, my phone finally rings. It's Lacey.

"Gabby, my parents are home finally. Can you come?"

Grandma watches on with a knowing look as I say,

"I'm already on my way."

Chapter 10

GABBY

Dustin's car is parked in Mr. and Mrs. Aniston's driveway when I pull in. I'm surprised he's still in his personal car, not a cruiser. I feel bad for the men. They've been up all night.

The house looms large, a monstrosity of red brick and white trim. I'm sure at one time, the overdone nature of the mansion was in style. The lion statues flanking the porch are a bit over the top for me.

My feet slow as I make my way to the wide front doors. I'm hoping Lucas isn't still sore at me. I'd rather see him in private, apologize again. Instead, I'll have to be on my best behavior to be professional.

A whiff of smoke carries across the porch, and Lacey

is on the far end, sitting on a swing.

"I'm glad you came," she says. Her face looks tired and I doubt she got any sleep at all last night either. I suddenly feel guilty for passing out on Grandma's couch.

"I want to help," I say as I approach the swing. "How are your parents?"

"Worried. Freaking. Desperate. Dad actually asked for you. 'We need that psychic girl,' were his exact words."

"Not sure what else I can do."

She stubs out the last of her cigarette and stands suddenly. "I do. Let's go to her old room and see if you can get a read on her again."

Lacey grabs my wrist and pulls me towards the front door. Her fingers are touching the bare skin above my glove. A tingle sizzles up my arm.

She drops my hand and rubs her palm against her hip. "You really are a freak, aren't you?" She sounds more curious and interested than judgmental.

I rub at my wrist. "It's you, too. And don't call me a freak or I'll walk out now."

She tosses her hair over her shoulder, "Whatever. Let's go." She opens the heavy door and I can hear Lucas inside talking to the parents. His voice makes me go warm but fills me with nerves.

I step towards the door on slow feet. Lacey notices. "He's a bit grouchy this morning. Maybe you can cheer him up while you're here." She smiles knowingly.

I don't like Lacey talking about Lucas. I raise my chin and step into the cavernous house.

Lucas sees me first and a smile flickers across his lips before he scrunches it. "Gabby?"

Anthony Aniston jumps to his feet, "You came. Thank you." He reaches towards me to shake my hand then obviously thinks better of it. He finally shoves his hands into his pants pockets.

"Mr. Aniston. I'm so sorry for what you're going through."

"Right, right. The detectives were just getting us up to speed on what's been done so far. Lacey said you helped last night. I wanted to hear from you what you saw."

I dart my eyes to Lucas and then to Dustin who's been glaring from across the table. "I don't know if it will help, but," I then tell them as much details as I can.

"You saw her in a room?" Jenna Aniston finally says. "That's what you got? That's it?"

I'm not prepared for the disbelief. They did call me

here. "And that there is more than one kidnapper. I get the feeling that the man I saw was a different man than the one I saw take her." I flounder.

"That's good news," Lucas says, coming to my rescue. "At least we know she wasn't taken by some sicko on his own."

"But who would take her?" Jenna asks the room. "Did you see his face? Anything that would lead us to him?" She asks me.

I shake my head. "It doesn't work like that."

She makes a sound of disgust. I let it slide.

"Let's go upstairs," Lacey says. "We're going to see if Gabby can sense anything from Aubry's old things. It worked with the cell phone last night."

Dustin opens his mouth in protest, but shuts it when Anthony says, "Yes, whatever you need to do."

I follow Lacey up the wide, marble stairs. I'm surprised at the opulence of the home. When we were growing up, I always knew Lacey had money, but I never realized how much. I'll take Grandma's homey farmhouse full of love over cold marble any day.

Lacey leads me down the hall to Aubry's room. The door is closed and she hesitates.

"I'm going to help you once we get in here, but you better not tell," she hisses.

"It's really not that big a deal," I say in my defense. "There are worse things than having the ability to see things."

"Right, because your life has been easy with your abilities." She opens the door and walks in.

I don't point out that she has been a leading contributor to my troubles, but follow her in.

I don't know Aubry well, but her childhood room is not what I pictured. I'd expected flowers and pinks. Instead, the walls are covered with posters of heavy metal bands. One wall is painted in black chalkboard paint and what looks like lyrics from her favorite songs are scribbled all over the wall.

I don't need my talent to sense the angst in these walls.

Lacey closes the door behind us. "So where do you want to start?"

I glance around the room looking for something truly personal. "You know this might not work. Looks like she hasn't used this room in a long time."

"Only about a year. She was here until she moved in with Brent."

Lacey is watching me intently and I feel her judging my inaction. Not knowing what else to do, I pull off my gloves. I open my hands, palm up and close my eyes hoping for guidance.

The room is silent.

"Lord, let me see what I need to see," I say out loud.

Still nothing.

I open my eyes. "I don't think this is going to work."

Lacey grips my bare palm, "Do it again."

I close my eyes and open myself to the universe. I feel a tingle between Lacey's slightly damp palm and mine. Then my tattoo sizzles.

ries Ke.

Lacey suddenly lets go of my hand. "What in the world?"

"Did you see that? The letters ries Ke?"

She pulls on a lock of her hair, "I saw something. What is ries ke?"

"No idea. Let's try it again." This time I pick up Aubry's pillow and hold it against my chest. Lacey's hand shakes as she takes mine again.

This time, I see the letters clearer. "I think it's a sign. Blue with white letters."

Lacey is breathing hard. "I see it. Is that what Aubry is seeing right now?"

The vision goes away and I feel empty and scared. "I don't know what it means."

She pulls on her hair again, twists it in her fingers. "This is so frustrating. Why can't we just see where she is, see who has her?"

A ringing phone saves me from answering. Lacey's head jerks up. "That's the land line. No one ever calls the land line." She hurries from the room and I toss the pillow back on the bed.

"Where are you?" I ask the empty room. The ringing phone is cut off mid-ring. I hear Anthony saying, "This is he." I hope it's a random telemarketer call, but I know it's not.

I make my way downstairs and notice that a table in the far end of the dining area is set up with equipment to record the call. For a moment, I feel like I'm on a television show. Anthony's desperate "Please don't hurt her. I'll pay whatever you want," brings the situation back to reality.

Aubry truly has been kidnapped.

And we just got the ransom notice.

Chapter 11

LUCAS

As much as I trust Gabby and her visions, I hoped she was wrong about Aubry being kidnapped. Bad enough Brent was dead. Better Aubry was safe and on the run than being held captive.

The ransom call solidifies it. Aubry is in trouble.

Anthony Aniston keeps his composure well as he talks to the kidnapper. We have the recording and tracing equipment running, something I'm glad I pressed for on the chance of this very phone call.

Unfortunately, the call doesn't last long enough to trace, but a time and amount is settled on.

One hundred thousand dollars at midnight at the old wooden bridge at River Bend Park.

Anthony hangs up the phone and repeats the instructions just as Gabby and Lacey come back into the room. Gabby is pulling her gloves back on, and Lacey is rubbing her hands together like she wants to wash them. I wonder what the two of them have been up to in Aubry's room and if it might help us find her.

"Well, that's that. We just have to wait until midnight and we'll get our daughter back," Jenna Aniston says.

"That's what we're all hoping for," Dustin says.

"That's what's going to happen," she says firmly.

"Can you get the money together?" I ask Anthony. Their house is grand, but one hundred thousand dollars in cash is a lot of money.

"I'll have to move some stuff around, but I think I can."

"We'll have it," Jenna says, standing up from the table. "We have to."

"We'll have men posted at the bridge, hidden. You'll be covered. Are you up to making the drop?" Dustin asks Anthony.

"I'll do whatever it takes." He rubs his hands together nervously. "Now if you will excuse me, I have to make some calls and get the money arranged." Aniston stands tall. He seemed like a broken man when we told him about Aubry a few short hours ago, now I see the titan of real estate that financed this fine home. He's used to commanding a room. "First, Ms. McAllister would you come with me."

Gabby looks surprised to be singled out. "Of course," she mumbles and follows him out of the room.

"I want to hear every detail of what you saw. Including anything you learned just now upstairs."

Jenna makes a small sound of disgust at Gabby's retreating back. "Like that will save her."

I school my face into a blank expression. Now is not the time to start waves by defending Gabby. I'm still miffed at her myself for her brazen acts last night.

"She actually has been very helpful," Lacey says, surprising me.

"You should have called the cops first, not her," Jenna says.

"You weren't there. I did what I could."

"And lost valuable time."

"The cops haven't helped, either. All we have is this phone call," Lacey says.

Dustin and I exchange looks and make our way for the front door. "We'll let you two discuss this. Gonna step outside for a moment," I say and go out onto the front porch.

The morning air feels wonderful on my tired face. I rub at my eyes. It's been a long night.

"How you want to play this?" Dustin asks. "Wait for the ransom drop or go look for her?"

"Probably safest to wait for the drop. If they just want the money, they'll keep her safe." Dustin rubs the back of his head in exhaustion. "Man, what I wouldn't give for a little sleep."

Mention of sleep makes me yawn. I cover my mouth with my hand but Dustin sees it. It makes him yawn, too, and we laugh a little.

"Detective Hartley?" Office Patterson is suddenly behind me on the porch steps.

Feeling like a kid caught laughing in church, I turn to face the officer. "What's up? I thought you were still working the neighborhood canvas?"

"I was, but Chief Simmons sent me to find you. We got the DNA back. Gomez wasn't kidding when she put the rush on it."

"The blood in the kitchen is Aubry's, right?" I ask, confused why they'd send Patterson to tell us and not just call with the info.

He looks at the papers in his hand as if they might bite him.

"That's true, but there's more," he hedges.

"Spit it out, Patterson, it's been a long night," Dustin says.

"The tests they ran on Gabby and Lacey," Patterson continues, "They match, or sort of match."

I feel Dustin bristle next to me. "What are you trying to say? They match what?"

"Each other." Patterson searches Dustin's face. "And your father."

Dustin grabs the papers and scans the reports. "Of course, Gabby will match Nathan."

"But so does Lacey's and Aubry's." Patterson takes a breath. "They are your half-sisters."

Dustin looks at me with disbelief and hands me the papers. "This doesn't make sense."

I scan the reports and it's there in black and white. Gabby, Lacey and Aubry are all daughters of Nathan McAllister. I already knew he'd had a long time affair with my mother, Deidre, looks like he and Jenna were closer than anyone thought.

The front door opens and Lacey huffs out. "Man, you'd

think mom blames me for what happened," she says. She picks up her pack of smokes from the table near the porch swing and lights one with her back to us.

We all stare at her with fresh eyes. She looks like her mom, all light and blond. Nathan has dark hair and blue eyes like Gabby and Dustin. I don't see a resemblance, but DNA doesn't lie.

She feels us staring at her and turns around. "What?"

Dustin just stares at her, so I do the talking. "Do you know if your mother and Nathan McAllister knew each other?"

She wraps an arm around her waist. "I suppose so. Doesn't everyone in this town know everyone?"

Dustin takes the DNA papers back from me. "Where's Gabby?"

"She's in talking with my Dad. He's quite interested in her talents. Sure she's going to single-handedly solve this whole thing."

Dustin goes inside.

"What's going on? You guys are acting cagier than normal."

"We got some news. I think it's best to wait for Gabby and your parents."

She stares me down hard. "Is it bad news about Aubry?"

"No," I assure her. "Nothing like that."

Dustin returns with Gabby and Lacey's parents, all three faces are full of interest and concern.

"Have you heard something already?" Anthony asks, pacing the porch.

I hold up the papers. "Last night we ran DNA on Gabby and Lacey and the blood we thought was Aubry's. We go the reports back this morning."

Jenna makes a small gasp of surprise mixed with fear. She covers her mouth with her hand and moans, "Oh, no."

Anthony looks at his wife in confusion. "So? What's the big deal?"

"I hate to be the one that has to break the news to you, but it looks like Nathan McAllister is the biological father of both Lacey and Aubry."

Gabby makes a strange sound and she leans against the porch rail. "That can't be possible," she mutters.

Jenna's face has turned a bright shade of red. Anthony swings to face her. "Is this true? You and McAllister? That murdering, embezzling, monster?"

Jenna covers her face with her hands and tears roll

from her eyes. "It was a long, long time ago. You were always working."

"I was working?" Anthony shouts. "That's what you have to say?"

"It was just the few times," she says miserably. "I swear, I didn't know they were his daughters."

"A few times and you didn't know?" Anthony bellows. He slams a fist into the porch railing. "How could you? And to keep it from me all this time."

"Anthony, I'm so sorry. Lacey?" Jenna searches for her daughter. Lacey has sunk into the porch swing far from our group.

"Don't talk to me," she says. "Dad, you are my dad. That's all that matters. This DNA crap is nothing."

"Except I have sisters," Gabby says quietly. "Sisters."

"I already have a sister," Lacey says coldly. "I don't need another."

Gabby's face crumbles.

"Maybe we should leave and let them discuss this in private," I say. I take Gabby's hand and lead her down the steps. Dustin follows silently.

I can't imagine what Anthony must be going through today. "We'll be back later to check on the ransom money and go over tonight's plan," I tell him.

He stares across the yard in a daze, but manages a nod.

"Right. One hundred thousand dollars for another man's daughter." I know it's the shock talking, but it tears my heart just the same.

A sick thought fills my heart. If Nathan fathered these girls with a woman he had an affair with, what about my mom? He was with her for years behind my father's back.

I squeeze Gabby's hand and search her face. Is there a possibility we are related too? We both have dark hair.

All thoughts of a nap have left my mind. The first thing I'm doing now is going to Gomez's lab and having her run a DNA on me. Our future depends on it.

Chapter 12

GABBY

Sisters?

I can hardly wrap my mind around the word. Not one but two. One of them has hated me until very recently and one of them is currently being held captive.

That's a lot to take in.

I focus on the strength in Lucas's hand as he leads me down the porch steps and to my car.

"Are you alright?" he asks as he opens the door to my Charger.

"I'm not sure." I look at Dustin. "What do you think about all this?"

"I think there's nothing that man can do that would surprise me anymore." He rubs at his shoulder where he was shot by our father a few months ago. "Can't wait until his trial is over and they lock him away in prison."

"But sisters? I mean, how will all this work?"

"They are not our sisters. He's just a sperm donor," Dustin snaps. "Lacey has been nothing but mean to both of us and Aubry we don't even know."

I look away from my brother. He's right. Until last night, Lacey has been downright horrid. Not sister-like at all.

"Poor Mom. Another blow from the world's worst husband. I think she's at the apartment. I better go tell her before she hears it through the rumor mill."

I expect Lucas to give me a kiss good-bye but he seems distracted. "Do you need me for anything before I go? I did see something while Lacey and I were upstairs. I don't know if it's helpful. Part of a sign maybe? Only letters. 'ries Ke' Does that mean anything to you guys?"

Dustin shakes his head. "We'll look into it, but nothing comes to mind." By his tone, I doubt he's going to do anything with the info. They are pretty focused on the ransom drop tonight.

I hesitate and look at Lucas, wondering why he's being so quiet. He can't still be mad at me about the phone last night can he?

"Well, then," I say. "Guess I'll go see Mom."

The men turn away, so I climb into my car and pull out of the wide driveway. Lucas's shoulders are slumped with concern. I tell myself he's worried about Aubry, not mad at me.

I almost believe it.

Mom's small white car is parked in the alley behind my shop "Messages" where I do readings on objects for people. After I solved a murder here a few weeks ago, business has been booming. Mom lives in the apartment upstairs.

I let myself in the back door and holler up the stairs to her door. "Mom, you here?"

Her door rattles and I see her smiling face in the crack of the door. I hate that I'm about to erase that smile.

"Gabby, I figured you'd be busy with that kidnap case today," she says as I go up the stairs.

"I was at the Aniston's already this morning. Not much more I can do at this point." Mom pulls me close for a hug. I notice it lasts a little longer than usual. I wonder about her living here alone. I am around a lot, but after she spent fourteen years wrongfully imprisoned, I imagine the nights get lonely with only goldfish for company.

"You added a picture of Walker, I see," I say looking at the walls of the living area of the apartment. She and Grandma Dot covered them in framed family photos. The effect is heart-warming.

"That baby boy has stolen my heart."

I nod. "He is a sweety," I hedge, not wanting to come to the point of my visit.

I look in on the goldfish, then pull the curtain back and look down on the town square. The courthouse sits across the street, people coming and going. On the far side of the square, I see a familiar form.

Alexis is walking into a door.

I've seen her in that part of town before. She doesn't have Walker with her, which is odd.

I don't have time to wonder what Alexis may be up to. She's a grown woman with her own life. I have bad news to deliver.

"Want to tell me why you are stalling?" Mom asks.

"I'm not stalling," I lie.

"Yes, you are. Whatever you're trying not to tell me, just get on with it."

"We got some news this morning," I sit on the couch and motion for Mom to join me. "They ran DNA tests on Lacey and her sister and me last night to rule us out of the crime scene."

Mom's lips purse in confusion. "Okay?"

"Well," I rub my gloved finger along the edge of the cushion, "Turns out Lacey, Aubry and I are sisters. Half-sisters."

Mom's mouth falls open then closes with a snap when she makes the connection. "The bastard!"

"Jenna Aniston admitted it," I say sadly.

"How could he? I mean, I suppose with everything else he's done to me. That woman, Diedre, the fake murder, shooting Dustin, killing those people, embezzlement, who know what else? Daughters? He has daughters?" Mom paces furiously around the room. "Does his depravity have no end? How could I have been married to that man?"

"He fooled us all, Mom," I say quietly, my heart breaking to see her so upset.

"But he was my husband. I should have known. I should have suspected or sensed something. How could I have been so stupid?"

"Stop that! You are not stupid. Not now and not then. He is evil. Plain and simple."

Mom stops pacing and stares at a picture of Dustin and me from when we were little. "At least I got you two from him. He did something good with his life."

I continue rubbing at the cushion, not sure what to say. She suddenly strides across the room and grabs her keys off the hook by the door.

"He won't get away with this without some sort of retribution," she nearly shouts. "Are they still holding him at County?"

"As far as know, he's there until his trial next month," I shoot off the couch and follow her down the stairs. "Where are you going?"

"That man has done so much to me. It's about time I confront him."

"Mom, you can't."

She spins on the bottom step. "Why not? He cheated on me with at least two women that we know of. He framed me for his murder and left me to rot in prison. And he shot my son," she adds dramatically. "He will hear what I have to say to him."

The look in her eyes tells me there's no way to talk her

out of it.

"Let me go with you."

"You sure you want to do this?" I ask Mom as we pull into the parking lot of the County Jail where my father is awaiting his trial. "Won't it bring back bad memories?" Mom spent months waiting in this jail for her own trial when she was framed for murder.

She raises her chin and stares straight ahead. "I'll be fine." I can only imagine what this must be like for her. She hasn't seen Nathan McAllister since the night he covered our kitchen in his blood and disappeared.

"Leave everything in the car," I tell her as we are climbing out. I visited her every month while she was locked away. I'm familiar with the procedure. She silently hides her phone and purse under the front seat of my Charger. Although I doubt anyone would break into a car parked at the jail.

We walk to the entrance without speaking. She pauses outside the thick glass doors and gives me a wry look. "Ready?" she asks.

I nod.

Mom takes a deep breath, grabs the handle of the

heavy door and pulls it open.

We go through the security checkpoint without issue and are soon waiting behind the Plexiglass partition. My nerves are jumping. I don't want to see my father, especially after hearing he cheated on my mother with yet another woman. It seems the deeds he's capable of are unbounded.

Mom's hands are shaking and I pat them in her lap. "We can still leave. You don't have to see him."

"No. I need to do this."

The other side of the glass fills with an orange jump suit and we are face to face with the man who has done everything he can to ruin our lives.

"Emily," he says. "They told me it was you, but I didn't believe them."

"Nathan," she says the one word bold and strong.

"Hey, Gabby Girl." The joy in his voice is evident and makes my skin crawl. "So glad to see you again."

"I'm not here to see you. I'm here to support Mom."

"But you are here. That says something." I don't like his smug tone. The man before me barely resembles the man I knew and loved as my dad. His hair has grayed and Grandma Dot would be appalled at the state of his hair cut. The flint in his eyes is the same, though.

"Jenna Aniston?" Mom asks. "Really?"

Nathan looks confused for a moment then he makes the connection. "Oh yeah, Anthony's wife. I remember her."

"Remember her? You did more than meet her at a party," Mom says. "You fathered two daughters with her."

"I did?" His surprise is obviously false. "How about that? Poor, pathetic, Anthony couldn't do the job. Someone had to help Jenna out."

"That's what you call it? Helping her out?" Mom's voice is rising and a few people are looking our way. I place a hand on her shoulder.

"Seriously, Emily. All that was a long time ago."

"Not for me. I just found out."

"Is that why you came here? Because of some fling I had with a bored rich woman years ago?" He smiles and I want to reach through the glass and slap it off his face.

Mom is silent a beat. "I'm not sure why I came here, exactly. I just wanted you to see that you didn't beat me. You framed me and stole years of my life. You shot my son and tried to take him away and failed. You cheated on me and fathered children with another woman. But here I am. I'm still standing. You always thought I was the weak one, the stupid one. The only stupid thing I've done in my life is trust you. But I won in the end. I'm on this side of that glass. I have Gabby and Dustin with me. You have nothing."

He leans back in his chair in a practiced motion of nonchalance but his eyes have tightened at the corners. "Big words from a woman I duped."

"You duped everyone."

He looks proud of himself. "I did, didn't I?"

I lean close to the glass. "That's not something to be proud of."

"And yet, I am, Gabby Girl." If my momma and Grandma Dot hadn't raised me better, I would have spit on the glass.

Mom puts her hand on my shoulder. "I've said all I need to say. Let's go."

We stand to go and he calls out as we walk away. "I'll see you soon, Gabby."

I spin around. "I won't be back. I'll never see you again."

He shrugs and smiles an enigmatic smile. Something in

me goes cold and my tattoo grows hot. I itch at it in confusion. The guard comes to take him back to his cell and he continues smiling at me. The burn grows hotter.

"Come on," Mom says. "Let's get out of here."

It's not until we are back outside in the bright sun that my blood warms again and my tattoo stops sizzling.

Chapter 13

GABBY

Mom keeps her eyes locked out the side window as we drive home from the jail, but I don't think she's seeing any of the lovely countryside sliding past. My mind is swirling with what we just did and how my tattoo burned. No words from God came, no directions. Just the burning.

We drive in silence until we cross the river back to town. I look down river towards the wooden covered bridge that is the center point of the town park and the place the kidnappers chose for ransom drop tonight. There're two figures under the bridge, fisherman maybe? Or members of the police force doing something to get ready for tonight?

"He looked old," Mom breaks the silence as we cross

back onto land. "In my mind, he still looked like he did the last time I saw him. I don't know why I didn't think that he'd be older now. That was years ago." She doesn't draw her eyes from the window and seems to be musing to herself. "Life has not been kind to him." She suddenly laughs. "Balding. Ha. He was always afraid of that. Hope all his gray hair falls out."

"He definitely is thinner on top, even than he was last fall," I agree.

"He deserves everything bad that can come his way," she says. "He thinks he has it bad now in County. Wait until he's convicted and sent to prison. That's when things really turn bad." Her voice trails off, no doubt thinking of the time she spent there. She suddenly shakes herself and smiles at me. "But those days are over."

"Over and gone," I agree. "Nothing but freedom for you now."

She squeezes my hand. "Thank you for coming with me."

I squeeze back. "I'm glad I went. Was a bit of closure for me, too."

"At least his philandering brought us some good. You have two sisters."

I take a deep breath. "I'm not sure how I feel about that, yet. It hasn't quite sunk in. Lacey was definitely not receptive to the idea that we were related. Said she didn't need another sister. Of course, it was a shock and she's under major stress today with Aubry missing."

"Who would take that girl for ransom? I mean everyone knows the Aniston's have money, but to kidnap their daughter? There must be a grudge involved, too."

"People do strange things for money," I point out. "I just hope tonight's exchange goes smoothly and no one gets hurt."

"You won't be there?"

"I'm not allowed anywhere near the case now." I fiddle with a worn spot on the steering wheel, not wanting to tell Mom about how I screwed up last night and made everyone mad at me.

She sees me fiddling. "What did you do?" she asks with a knowing tone.

"Let's just say, my presence would not be appreciated right now." I pull into the alley behind my shop and Mom's apartment. "Besides, I have clients this evening."

Mom, thankfully, lets it go without me having to confess my sins.

"You'll do what you need to," she says and climbs out of the car.

I follow her to the door and she lets us in. I'm suddenly hungry and realize the toast Grandma Dot gave me was hours ago. "You got anything to eat?" I ask.

Mom laughs. "I wondered how long it would take for you to ask. We should have gotten something while we were out."

"I did a reading at the Aniston's this morning," I defend myself as I follow her up the steps to the apartment.

"I have some of Grandma's rice Krispy treats, will that do? And I could make you a sandwich."

"You're the best." I head right to the small kitchen and take one of the delicious treats. "This should do."

The sun is shining through the living room window and is warm on my back. The moment is as sweet as the Krispy treat. I can't help comparing this moment with Mom with all the visits I made to her in prison.

Despite the danger Aubry may be in, and the fact that my boyfriend and brother are barely talking to me, today has been a good day. I said good-bye forever to the man I despise and I found out I have two sisters.

Now we just have to pay to get the one sister back.

I fill the rest of the day with my clients. I keep checking the clock on my phone and mentally calculating the time until the ransom drop. I also hope the phone will show me that Lucas has called or texted and I somehow just missed it. I turn my phone off during client visits, so it's possible he'd call and I'd miss it.

He doesn't call.

I hope he's home getting some much needed rest before tonight. He's been up since yesterday morning. I worry about him when he works such long hours. He tells me it's all part of the job. I think he'd work better if he was rested once in a while.

That's one of the many reason's I'd make a bad cop. I need my sleep.

Especially after doing readings. Between the many readings I did at the crime scene and the short night on Grandma's couch, I woke up depleted. After doing client readings all day, I'm wiped.

The sun is dipping low when I see my last client to the door. I just manage to stifle a yawn as I show them out and lock the door behind them. I turn my phone on again and check for messages.

One text from Grandma Dot, "Emily told me you have sisters! Call me!" Grandma loves exclamation points in texts.

I'm too tired to talk about it now and truly I still don't know how I feel about it. On the one hand, it changes nothing. Lacey still will probably hate me, even after asking for my help. Aubry is a stranger to me. Dustin is a pain in my butt. I can't imagine having two half sisters will change any of that.

Still, it might be nice. When I was growing up, Lucas's sister Crystal was the closest thing I had to a sister. That didn't turn out well.

My friend, Haley, is more of an acquaintance now that we don't work together. She drops into the shop once and a while, but we aren't really close.

I realize that blood won't make Lacey and Aubry my dear friends or anything, but maybe a relationship could grow there.

I sit at my desk and stare out at the town hall in the square, all lit up and lovely. I suddenly feel lonely. Yes, Mom is upstairs. Yes, Grandma Dot is waiting for me to call. I have Lucas and he is wonderful. But he's not talking to me right now.

Maybe a sister or two would be great. Of maybe they will just be someone else to argue with like Dustin. Of course, I know Dustin loves me and I argue as much as he does. I wouldn't give him up for the world.

I suddenly know exactly how I feel about having sisters. I'm excited.

I pick up the phone and text Grandma Dot. "I'm excited about it and what it might mean for our family. You always said, family is family, no matter what shape it comes in. I'll call you in the morning."

She texts right back. "Get some sleep. Proud of you."

I tingle at the praise.

An hour later, I've wrapped up the paperwork for today's clients, cleaned my desk and even dusted behind my computer. I can't think of anything else to do to fill the time before the ransom drop. I can't bring myself to go home. I feel left out. I know they have good reason for me not to be involved and truly I don't know what I could do to help. I just feel like I should be there.

I sweep the floors in my shop and fluff the pillows on the yellow couch.

I check the time. Still two hours to go.

I clean the front windows until they sparkle then have no idea what else to do. I stare out the clean windows at the court house. The square is deserted at this time of night. All the businesses have long ago closed for the day, their lights out. My lights are normally turned out hours ago.

"I thought I heard you rummaging around down here," Mom suddenly says from behind me. I was so absorbed in staring out the window and worrying about Aubry I didn't hear her come downstairs.

I spin, startled, grabbing my chest. "You scared me," I accuse.

"You scared me. I thought maybe someone broke in or something. I figured you'd be home in bed by now."

"I'm worried about Aubry and the drop tonight. I wish I knew what was going on."

Mom looks around the spotless shop. "Looks like you've been busy."

"I clean when I'm nervous."

"You should come upstairs, I could find something for you to clean," she teases.

"I should probably go home and clean my own house. I think I've done all I can here."

I check my phone again, I've managed to fill some more time. "Just over an hour now until the drop. She's going to be okay, right?"

"Of course, baby." Mom takes me into her arms for a quick hug. I settle into the embrace for a precious moment then let her go. "You can worry just as well from home. I'm sure Lucas will let you know how it goes."

"I'm not so sure. He's pretty upset with me."

"That's only temporary. That boy loves you. Nothing's going to change that." A huge yawn suddenly takes over my face. "See, you're exhausted. Go home and rest and this will all be over soon. Aubry will be home."

I decide to listen to my mom and go home. I'm not helping anyone here, just keeping mom up.

I start driving towards home, but it's like the Charger has its own mind and I find myself at the park. The wooden covered bridge is deserted and so is the parking lot. I take the spot under a tree and as far from the bridge as possible and turn off the car. To anyone watching I'm just a townsperson out to stargaze, or whatever someone does in the middle of the night at a park. Hopefully, no one is watching. The entire place is deserted. Mine is the only car here.

I sit and watch the bridge, not sure why I've come, knowing I'm not allowed. My tattoo tingles and I listen gratefully.

Wait.

I blow out air in relief. If God wants me here, then nothing will stop me. If my own curiosity was the only thing that brought me here, that's another problem.

So I wait, munching on caramels I find in the center console. My eyes scan the park on both sides of the bridge, but I don't see anyone. If there are police coming to the drop, they either aren't here yet or are too well hidden. As the minutes drag on my imagination takes over and I feel eyes all around me. Is that a branch in that tree or a sniper? Is that bush extra wide? Did I see movement under the bridge?

I focus on that movement. Seriously, something is moving under the bridge on the far side of the river.

As I watch a man climbs from under the bridge and up the far bank.

My tattoo zings so hard, I cry out in pain.

He turned it on.

Now, what does that mean? I watch the dark figure until it disappears into the brush on the far side of the river.

My tattoo is burning, insistent.

Only you can stop it.

A Cadillac pulls into the park, drawing my attention away from my arm. I recognize the car as Anthony Aniston's.

The drop time is here.

Anthony parks so his headlights illuminate the bridge. He takes a few moments to just watch the bridge. Someone moves at the far end. Two dark figures are holding a young blond, presumably Aubry, between them.

My blood pounds. This is happening.

Anthony climbs out of the Cadillac with a heavy bag and makes his way towards the bridge.

My tattoo sizzles.

Stop him. Stop him. Stop him.

I rub my arm and beg it to be quiet. "Not now."

Don't let Anthony on the bridge.

Clear words. No guessing at the message.

"Lord let me be doing the right thing," I whisper as I pull open my car door.

Anthony's almost to the bridge when he hears me. He spins around, startled.

I run across the parking lot towards him.

At the far end of the bridge, the two dark figures are still holding Aubry, but I notice they are not on the bridge but on the lane before it.

"Gabby? What in the world are you doing here? You're ruining everything!" Anthony whispers loudly.

Chapter 14

GABBY

Anthony is not happy to see me and I have no way of explaining why I'm here. He may believe in my gift, but he won't understand about the messages from my tattoo.

"You can't go on the bridge," I say lamely.

"I have to. There's Aubry. I have the money. This will be over in a minute. Just go away."

My arm aches from the burning, the message to keep him from the bridge blaring in my head. I am helpless but to obey it.

I pull on his arm, a feeble attempt to keep him back. He shakes me off and I fall to the grass. "Stop, Gabby. What's gotten into you?"

"I had a vision," I say, desperate. "Something bad will happen to you on the bridge."

He glances at Aubry at the other side of the river, her eyes huge with fear. "Something worse will happen if I don't."

He hurries onto the bridge, his shoes loud against the wooden planks. Aubry pulls forward, but the two masked men hold her back.

I get to my feet and follow him. When we reach the center of the bridge, I'm close enough to grab his shirt and pull.

He's seriously angry now. "Let go now." Each word is distinct.

"I can't," I say miserably.

My arm sizzles and the message changes.

Jump, jump, jump.

I look over the side of the bridge to the rolling river below.

"We have to jump," I beg.

"I'm not jumping! Go away. Lacey is right, you're crazy."

I pull his arm towards the side of the bridge, but he's taller and stronger than I am.

"Listen, if you believe in my abilities at all, even a little, you'll do what I say. I have a vision. We have to jump."

I climb onto the rail and shockingly, he follows.

I balance on the old wood and look at the water rushing under us.

Now, now, now.

I grab Anthony's hand and scream, "Now!" I step from the railing and pull him with me.

The water is shockingly cold as it envelops me. My lungs clamp and my body aches. I kick for the surface.

"What the--?" Anthony shouts as he surfaces next to me.

His words are cut off by the explosion.

I duck underwater, a futile attempt to take cover.

When I resurface, I'm farther downriver. Shards of wood rain down on us and fire licks at what remains of the bridge.

Anthony's eyes are wide with shock, the flames reflected in them. "How did you know?" he asks in awe.

"I had a vision," I tell him again kicking to stay afloat in the current. "I didn't know it was a bomb, I just knew you were in danger." I can hardly say the words, my teeth are chattering so badly.

He treads water, the heavy bag of money pulling him down. "You saved my life," he chatters back.

"Only if we get out of this cold water." A heavy shiver

shakes me.

"What about Aubry?" He scans the lane on the far side of the river. The men and Aubry are gone.

"She wasn't on the bridge. I think they took her away again."

We swim for the bank. Only when my feet can touch do I notice the police swarming the area. I was right, they were in hiding.

Lucas is the first one to reach us. The burning bridge illuminates his face and his expression. A mixture of anger and fear.

"Gabby, this time you have gone too far," he says as he reaches to help me out of the river.

As the spring night air touches my wet skin, I shiver violently. "I saved Anthony," I point out.

"And nearly got yourself blown up. You shouldn't even be here," he shouts.

Dustin is suddenly by his side. There's only a touch of fear in his eyes, but plenty of anger.

"You can't stay out of trouble for one night? You were told not to come."

Anthony comes to my rescue. "I think we're all missing the point that she saved me. If she hadn't made me jump, I'd have been on that bridge."

We all look at the flaming remainders of River Bend's historic marker and the shouts turn to solemn silence for a moment.

"Did they take Aubry away?" I break the silence.

"They pulled her away before the bridge blew. They must have known," Lucas says. "But why blow up the bridge? They would have blown up the money, too."

"And me," Anthony adds.

"Of course. I'm just saying, if you were the target, why the ransom demand?"

Someone hands Anthony and me towels and I wrap it around me gratefully, wishing Lucas would hold me or at least look my way. "Maybe Anthony has been the target the whole time," I say, drying my face.

"Any idea who would want you dead or ruined?" Dustin asks.

Anthony is rubbing his hair with the towel, thinking. "It's possible I've made some enemies in my business dealings, but I find it hard to believe that anyone would go to this extent to get back at me." He points to the bridge that the fire department is now desperately trying to save.

"What about Aubry?" Anthony asks. He's still holding the bag of cash. "If they don't want money for her, how are we to get her back? There were two men holding her. That added to the bomb shows there's more than just a simple kidnapping going on here. What do you think?" He asks me. "Are you getting any more visions like you did about the bridge?"

"Visions about the bridge?" Lucas asks. I avoid his eyes but rub at my arm to let him know it was a message from my tattoo that warned me.

He makes a sound of disgust and turns to walk away. I watch his retreating back with a breaking heart. Dustin looks at Lucas then back to me, a slight look of surprise on his face.

"Anthony, we need to get you dried off and checked out. Then we need to figure out what to do next." Dustin says and they both follow Lucas away.

I'm left alone on the bank of the river, the sounds of crackling wood, spraying hoses and rolling river surround me. I suddenly feel like crying as the adrenaline fades away. No one offered to have me checked out for injuries, no one is including me in the plans.

"Thanks, Gabby," I whisper to myself sarcastically.

"Couldn't do this without you."

I leave the river and go to my car. I sit on the towel to protect my cracked leather upholstery and drive myself home. I turn the heat up full blast, but it doesn't stop the shivers.

Chester, at least, seems happy to see me. I rub his head in hello, then change into warm pajamas. I curl around him in my bed that seems even emptier now that I've gotten used to spending the nights with Lucas.

After a while, the shivering stops and I drift off to sleep.

Only to be woken later by a voice I never expected to hear again.

"Gabby, Girl. Well done," it says from the chair in the corner of my room.

Chapter 15

GABBY

I slide back against the headboard in surprise, my knees pulled up to my chin and the blanket wrapped around me. My father has been watching me sleep, has snuck into my room. I feel violated and scared.

"How are you here?" I ask with as much bravado as possible. If he wanted to hurt me he would have done it already. Of course, he shot Dustin in cold blood, so there's no telling what he's capable of.

He laughs softly. "I told you I would see you again soon this afternoon. I'm just keeping my promises."

"Your promises mean nothing and that doesn't explain why you are not in the jail where you belong."

"I admit, your visit today put a slight kink in my plans to escape, but I've found there is little I can't coerce or buy someone to do for me."

"But how?"

"Don't be tedious. The details don't matter."

"You'll never get away with this."

He stands and turns on the light switch. "I spend enough time in the dark, I prefer the light." Chester crouches and hisses at him.

"Cute cat," he says sarcastically.

I want to hiss along with Chester. "You haven't told me why you are here. If you escaped, you should be long gone. Lucas and Dustin will find you." I scan the room, looking for my phone. It's not on the night stand. I must have left it in the kitchen.

"You won't tell them. At least, not yet."

I jerk my chin up, "And why is that?"

"Because I have an offer for you."

"You don't have anything I want."

He lifts his hands and looks around the shabby room with the non-matching furniture and dirty laundry piled high. "Are you truly happy living like this? I can offer you so much more."

I make a sound of disgust, "And I'd have to break the law. You don't know me very well, but I uphold the law, put the bad guys away. I have no interest in becoming like you."

"You didn't follow the law earlier tonight," he says quietly.

I bristle at that. "Tonight was different."

"I set that bomb for you to find. You don't think I know you very well, but you're wrong. I know you better than you know yourself. I've studied you."

A bad feeling slithers up my spine. "What do you mean studied me?"

He sits on the edge of my bed and the mattress sags. "Do you really think there are so many people needing readings at your shop? This is a small town and your talents are very specific. How do you think you've been staying in business?"

It takes a moment for that to sink in. "You've been sending the clients?"

"I can do a lot from jail. All I need is access to a phone and a loyal team. This small town police force has no idea how deep my reach is into this town. Yes, I sent clients. Lots of them. They watch what you do and report back to me."

He suddenly grabs my wrist and pulls my arm to him. "This right here is the key." He runs a fingertip over my cross tattoo. My skin crawls at his touch.

I pull my arm away. "You don't know what you're talking about."

Is my business really a sham? Does he truly understand about the tattoo?

"Next Monday, you have an appointment with a Mrs. Clayton. She found a necklace in a dresser she bought at a garage sale. She wants you to figure out the history of it."

I blink in disbelief. "How do you know that?"

"Simple. I hired her. The necklace is old, and I'm sure you will find some history in it."

I want to be sick. I have been pleasantly surprised by the volume of clients I have had. It never occurred to me that they might be fakes. How good am I if I can't tell fake clients from real ones?

"Why? Why would you do that to me?"

"I didn't do it to you I did it for you. Don't you understand yet? You are worth more than all this you're living with right now. You are special, Gabby. You could use your gifts for so much more than that old shop and helping the inept River Bend Police."

"That police force includes your son."

"I no longer have a son," he says with disdain. He

suddenly smiles, "Besides, I have three daughters."

I want to smack the smile. "Have you known all this time about Lacey and Aubry being from you?"

"I had my suspicions. Jenna said they were having trouble getting pregnant. I just figured I'd help her out."

"So you did it to be helpful. How noble," I say sarcastically.

"No. Mostly, I did it to get back at Anthony. I never liked him."

I shake my head in disgust. "And tried to blow him up tonight?"

"Oh, Gabby. You still don't get it do you? I knew you'd show up there, you can't help yourself. I also knew that you'd sense there was trouble and save him. He was in no danger."

"But I was in danger, too. You can't control everything."

"My man was instructed not to detonate until you were safe and off the bridge. I have to say watching you jump into the river was quite a rush. I'm proud of you."

"You were there?"

"Of course."

"So the ransom drop was just to make me look

stupid?"

"Not stupid. Brave, determined. You'll do whatever needs done. I do the same thing. We are alike in so many ways."

"I am not like you," I say slowly, clearly.

He tries to meet my eyes and for a moment I'm taken back to my childhood when I looked up to him, thought he was the best man in the world. It was all a lie. I look to Chester who is still bristling next to me to avoid my father's eyes.

"Why did you kill Aubry's boyfriend?"

He leans towards me. "That boy was not nice to her. He got what he deserved."

"How noble. Protecting your secret daughter. What about Aubry?" I ask. "When will you return her?"

"I still want my money. I have resources, but spending Anthony Aniston's money will be sweet."

"Why do you hate him so much?"

"You won't like it." He stands and the bed squeaks.

"I don't like anything you do."

"He stole Jenna from me years ago."

I didn't expect this. I wouldn't imagine the man was capable of that kind of feeling.

"What about Mom?" The words pop out.

"I loved her, too, in a way. She was easy to care for."

"But you cheated on her several times and then put her in prison for your murder," I sneer.

He shrugs and it's all I can do to not fly at him. "Like I said, she was easy. Easy to love, easy to frame."

This time I bounce out of the bed and punch against his chest. "Get out of my house!"

He laughs, and holds my hands away from him. I don't have gloves on and the skin on skin contact sizzles.

Sickness swims through my belly. A darkness swirls, fills my mind.

My knees buckle but he holds me up, refuses to let go.

"This is what I mean. You're reading me right now. If you worked with me, we could do great things."

"Never," I whisper weakly. The darkness in him consumes my senses. "Please let me go."

He suddenly releases me and I crumple to the floor. He squats next to me, brushes my hair out of my face with a gentle touch.

"You really are amazing, aren't you, Gabby Girl?"

I don't feel amazing. I feel like I might puke.

He stands to leave.

"Wait," I say. "What about Aubry? How do we get her back?"

"Easy. I just want Anthony's money. I won't hurt her. Come find her. I have no doubt you'll figure it out. If that stupid brother and boyfriend of yours will let you."

"This is really just a game to you, isn't it?"

"Oh, Gabby. All of life is a game." He leaves the room and walks into the hall.

"Say hello Grandma Dot for me," he says before the front door slams shut.

I take a few deep breaths then go to find my phone in the kitchen.

It's late, after 3:00 am. Still, I dial Lucas. It rings and rings, then goes to voicemail.

"Crap on a cracker," I mutter and press dial again.

This time he picks up. "Gabby, I'm really not in the mood right now," he grumbles sleepily.

"My father was just here. He's escaped."

This wakes him up.

"We'll be right there."

Chapter 16

LUCAS

I've been up for forty hours and in bed for less than an hour when Gabby's ring tone wakes me.

I don't want to answer it. I let it go to voicemail, too tired to deal with the drama tonight.

It rings again immediately.

My heart beats faster. I can't tell if it's from still being angry with her or excitement that she finally called

I decide it's both and answer the phone, irritated with myself.

I take my irritation out on her. "Gabby, I'm really not in the mood right now."

She doesn't say hello. She doesn't say she's sorry. She doesn't tell me she misses me.

She says, "My father was just here. He's escaped."

Nathan McAllister should be in jail, not haunting

Gabby's at night.

"We'll be right there," I say. I hang then bring up Dustin's name. I hesitate to dial. He's hasn't slept, either. I could take the report alone.

I shake my head in disgust, knowing I secretly want to see Gabby alone. Want to give her the chance to apologize for putting herself in danger and messing up the ransom drop.

She didn't blow up that bridge, and she saved Anthony.

I push that thought away. She should have been home safe in bed not at the park in the first place. I told her not to come. She was home in bed but not safe when Nathan showed up.

She nearly blew herself up.

I push that thought away, too. My greatest fear.

Frustrated at my swirling emotions, I stab the screen of my phone and call Dustin.

He sounds like I woke him, but manages a slurred, "This better be important."

"Gabby just called," I start. I can practically hear his eyes roll.

"I don't need to be part of your relationship issues. We can talk about it in the morning."

"It's not like that. And for the record, I don't need your help with relationships."

"What did my trouble-causing sister want at four in the morning?"

"She said your father was at her house."

"He's in jail awaiting trial."

"Apparently we have an escapee in town. Meet me at her house."

I toss off the blankets that have barely had time to warm and put on my uniform. We were allowed a few hours to rest before we were to report back in the morning. The few hours will have to wait.

I splash water on my face in an attempt to wake up. Some of it runs down the front collar of my shirt and ripples uncomfortably down my chest.

"Come on, Hartley, get it together," I grumble. I grab a towel and dab it at my chest. I dry under my shirt as well as I can then toss the towel on the floor in anger.

I have to see her.

I'm not sure I want to. Not sure I can act professional and not want to kiss her, or talk some sense into her, or rail at her in anger.

Checking my reflection, my eyes are red and droopy

and I need to shave. I search two drawers before I find the eye drops. I blink at the liquid's slight sting and consider a quick shave.

"Stop stalling," I say to the mirror. "She's not going to bite you."

This makes me laugh, way too hard. I laugh all the way to the car, glad it's the middle of the night so none of my neighbors can hear me.

Gabby's neighborhood is dark except for her house. She's turned on every light, including the front porch light. Her house glows.

I park on the street out front instead of in her driveway. This is the first major fight we've had since we officially started dating and I'm not sure how to act.

"You haven't actually fought yet," I tell myself. "Not really."

I've seen how she fights with her brother and I don't want to be on the receiving end of that. Talking things out logically is more my style. Of course, my first marriage imploded, so maybe logic isn't the right tactic.

Her form fills the front window and she pulls the curtain aside and looks out. I can't see her features but my heart stirs at her outline. I shake my head at myself. "Just stay professional."

Seeing me, she steps outside and waves excitedly. Luckily, Dustin pulls in so I don't have to face her alone.

We climb out of our cars at the same time. He's dressed in pajama pants and a t-shirt. I feel a little silly for being in full uniform.

"Dressed for the occasion, I see," he says with a grin. "You might need that vest if you plan on talking to her about the little stunt she pulled earlier tonight."

"Maybe you should talk to her about it."

"Let's take care of my illustrious father's latest crime first."

I nod and follow him up the walk to a waiting Gabby.

She tucks an unruly curl behind her ear and says, "Oh, my gosh, Dustin. It was really him."

"I called in to check and he was not in his cell. They didn't even know he was missing yet."

"He was there earlier today." She says. I look at her expectantly, waiting for the rest of that story.

"What?" she says. "So mom and I went to see him. She was upset about him cheating on her with yet another woman on top of all that he's done. She wanted to confront him and I wasn't letting her go alone."

"You went to see him in jail?" Dustin demands. "Are you nuts?"

She straightens her shoulders in agitation. I brace for her response, but she calmly says, "Yes. Yes, I did."

"And you think it's just a coincidence that later he escapes?"

"It is a coincidence. It's not like he just decided to escape and walked out. That type of thing takes time to set up. Besides, this isn't about what Mom and I did. This is about Aubry. He's the one behind her kidnapping."

"He said that?" I ask.

She nods and tucks the misbehaving curl behind her ear again. "He says he took her to get back at Anthony. Said he was in love with Jenna and hated Anthony." She stares across the yard into the darkness. I can tell she isn't giving us the whole story.

"Does he know he fathered the girls?" I hate thinking about the DNA link. I got the results from the test I had Gomez run comparing me to Gabby. Nathan had a long time affair with my mom, too. I look a lot like my father, so I know it's a long shot but I couldn't take the chance that Gabby and I were siblings.

Luckily there was no connection with our DNA.

Just thinking of how it could have been different makes my stomach roll.

"He knew all along," she says. "I think it gave him some sick satisfaction knowing he did that to Anthony."

"What does he want with Aubry?" I ask.

She looks into the dark again, holding back. "She isn't in real danger," she finally says. "He isn't going to hurt her."

"Why does he have her? If it was for money, he wouldn't have tried to blow up Anthony while he still had the cash on him."

"It isn't just for money," she hedges.

"You know more than you are saying," I tell her. "Did you have a vision or something?"

I meant it sincerely, but she snaps her eyes at me in anger.

"I didn't have a vision," she sneers the last word. "He told me what his plans are."

"Then tell us." I feel my anger stirring.

"You won't like it," she hedges.

"Look, we are tired and there's a girl in danger. I'm not in the mood for your cryptic answers tonight," Dustin snaps.

She crosses her arms across her middle.

"He said this is a test for me. He will hold her until I can find her. He thinks it's a game."

"A game he's playing with you?" I ask, appalled and concerned.

"It's not like I want to play," she snaps. "He's sick. But I have to find her."

"Or the police can find her. That is what we do," Dustin retorts.

"He doesn't believe you can."

"Do you?" I ask, suddenly furious. Does she really think she's better skilled at dealing with a kidnapping than the police are? How dare she?

"Of course not." Her words don't ring true. "You do realize that I help sometimes, right?"

That stings. It really stings.

"Dustin, did you know that we are just bumbling idiots that can't solve crimes without her?"

Dustin looks at me in surprise. I'm surprised, too. This conversation is not going the way I expected.

"Why don't we stay on track here," Dustin says. "Do you know why he blew up the bridge?"

Even in the pale light from above the front step, I can see her blush. "Another test," she says quietly. "He knew I'd be called to help and that I would come."

"How did he know?" I demand, angry that this man, who is basically a stranger to her, knew she'd come and I didn't.

She shrugs, "He just did. I don't know. He said he's had people watching me, studying me." She holds her elbows, squeezing herself. "Even most of my clients have been stooges of his. He has contacts everywhere." She shivers in the night air and goosebumps raise on her bare arms. Despite my anger, I long to hold her, to warm her, to tell her it's all going to be okay.

I'm not sure it is going to be okay. I'm not sure about anything right now. I rub at my eyes, wishing I had some more eye drops, I'm so tired. "Did he say anything else? Like where he's staying or how to get in touch with him?"

"No. It's not like I'm part of his gang. He just wants me to be," she snaps.

"Part of his gang? That's what he's after?" I practically shout.

"He thinks I could be a great help to him." She raises her chin in defiance.

"You'd help him?" Dustin asks in shock.

"Of course not. But it is nice to be asked for help instead of ridiculed about helping."

"We've asked for your help before," Dustin tries to placate her.

"That's different. You never want to. At least he wants me, needs me."

"You can't be serious?" I say.

"I said I would never help him." She looks across the yard again, "It's just been a long couple of days. Let's leave it at that."

She rubs at her tattoo and I wonder if she's getting something from it or if she even knows she's touching it.

"Are you getting something right now?" I ask, motioning to her arm.

"No." I can tell she's lying.

"What does it say?" I ask.

I check Dustin's reaction, but he seems to understand. I'm surprised he knows about the tattoo and the messages she gets from it.

"Is it about Aubry?" Dustin asks.

She suddenly bursts into tears. "I don't want to," she says under her breath and rubs her arm furiously.

Chapter 17

GABBY

I soon realize that it was a mistake to call Lucas about my father. I could just as easily have called 911 and reported it. A tiny part of me was hoping seeing Lucas would give him a chance to apologize.

As soon as I see him in uniform, I know he's going to be all cop tonight, not my dear Lucas.

I can play that game, too. I do pretty well at it until my tattoo starts tingling and giving me a message I don't want to hear.

Get rid of him. He's no good for you.

I don't understand. I want to make up with him, not get rid of him. This is just a blip in our relationship.

Lucas notices me rubbing my arm.

"Are you getting something right now?" he asks.

"No." I lie.

"What does it say?" he asks seriously.

Break up with him now.

Demanding and clear.

"Is it about Aubry?" Dustin asks.

Tears sting my eyes. "I don't want to," I tell God.

I can't disobey.

"I think you should go," I say to Lucas, meeting his tired eyes

"Yeah, we need to get looking for Nathan."

I swallow and try again, the words like poison on my tongue.

"No. I mean, we're over." I reach behind my neck and unclasp the necklace he gave me for Christmas. The one I have not taken off since he put it there. My neck feels bare without it.

When I hold it out to him, he slowly takes it, his eyes wide with shock. "You don't mean that."

I rub my tattoo, as *break up with him* pounds through my head.

My eyes are wet, but I must obey.

"I do mean it," I say desperately.

"Is your tattoo telling you to say this?" he asks gently.

I nod slowly. "We have to break up."

"Is that what you want?"

"It doesn't matter what I want," I choke out.

"You're really doing this based on some message from some ink in your arm?"

"It's a message from God," I try to explain. "I can't go against God."

He throws his arms wide, looks at Dustin. "I'm done," he says. "I can't do this anymore."

I wipe at my eyes. "Fine. Then that's it."

"Seriously, Gabby. That's it? You choose that over me?" he points to my arm.

I have no response.

"Better I know now," he says. "Come on, Dustin. We've been asked to leave." He turns and hurries down the walk to his car.

I want to call him back. I want to say it's all a mistake.

My tattoo keeps me quiet.

"Did you really just do that?" Dustin asks angrily.

"Stay out of it," I say.

Lucas starts his car and drives away. I feel like he's taking part of me with him.

I've never doubted God's messages before, but this one is too big.

Dustin shakes his head in disgust. "You're unbelievable." A few moments later Dustin drives away, too.

I sink to the front steps, my soul feeling like it's been torn in two.

I reach for the necklace that isn't there. My arm has stopped tingling and I can almost believe the last few minutes were a bad dream.

Except they weren't. God tore us apart and I don't know why.

"Lord, I've never doubted you before, but this time I think you have it wrong. Please be wrong. I may be upset with him tonight, but I love him."

I wait for a tingle, words in my mind, some sort of answer.

The night bugs are all I hear.

I sit on the step and put my head in my hands. I let the sobs shake me in the pre-dawn darkness. From next door, at Preston's house, comes a rumble. The sun is just beginning to touch the horizon. I'm surprised he's up and about. As a car salesman, he's not usually a super early bird.

Preston rolls his trash bin to the end of his driveway. He's dressed in pajama pants and a t-shirt. Not leaving for work.

"Crap on a cracker," I say, remembering today is trash day and my bin sits by the garage, my kitchen trash can overflowing and needing taken out.

I hope Preston will go back inside without seeing me, but he spies me as he comes back up his driveway.

"Gabby? You're up early."

I quickly wipe my eyes, not wanting my ex-boyfriend to find me crying. "I, uh, yeah, I am." I have no idea how to explain why I'm out on my step. I can't tell him about my early morning visitor.

"Did I just see the police here?"

"Dustin and Lucas were just here," I hedge. "They left"

Preston crosses from his driveway over mine and up the short sidewalk to where I sit. "Everything okay?" His concern is genuine.

I want to say no, everything is a mess, but I climb to my feet and say, "Police business," instead.

He shuffles uncomfortably. Despite being neighbors,

we have managed not to spend any time alone together since the night he left me after I told him about the messages from my tattoo.

"You look upset," he says, taking a step closer.

Tears suddenly burn on my cheeks and I wipe at them angrily. "I just broke up with Lucas." I hadn't meant to say the words, let alone to Preston. Saying them now makes it seem real and my heart shatters a little more.

He seems surprised. "Really? Why?"

I stiffen.

"I mean, you don't have to tell, me of course. It's just, you two seemed so happy together."

"We were," I sniffle.

"Then I don't get it." He looks down the road where Lucas recently drove away. "He didn't hurt you did he?"

"Of course not!" I instantly come to Lucas's defense. "He'd never hurt anyone."

Preston holds his hands wide and grins. "It's obvious you still care about him. Why did you break up with him?"

"Why do you want to know?" I hedge.

"Despite how we ended, I still care about you. I only want the best for you, and he seemed like the real thing."

"He was," I say miserably and rub my arm.

Preston's eyes widen. "It was the tattoo, wasn't it?"

I'm surprised he made the connection. "It told me to do it."

He shuffles again, this time in agitation. "You really believe in all that stuff, don't you?"

I stiffen. "Of course, I believe in all that stuff," I say sarcastically.

"Even though it has destroyed two relationships now?"

"I have to do what it tells me. What God tells me."

Preston blows out air in frustration. "Even if it hurts you?"

I nod. "He gave me these gifts, and I must obey them."

Preston shakes his head slowly. "You are a mystery, Gabby. On the one hand you are the most head-strong, stubborn woman I've ever known. On the other, you blindly obey messages that you assume are from God. You do know the Devil is very sneaky, right?"

I rub my arm again. "What do you mean?"

"Maybe not all the messages are from God." He stares me straight in the face now. I have to look away.

"They always have been."

"Maybe. I just think blind obedience is a dangerous

thing. I'd hate for you to ruin something good because of it."

I pull up the sleeve of my jacket and look at the delicate cross on my skin. It is not tingling or giving me any guidance now. I touch it with the tip of my bare finger, really look at it.

"It has never failed me before."

Preston shrugs. "Maybe I'm wrong. You know what you're doing." He shuffles again, changes the subject. "Do you want me to take out your trash bin? The truck will be here soon. It always comes super early. I forgot mine last night. I woke up and remembered it just now."

I'm glad he dropped the tattoo talk. "I'll get it, but thanks."

"See, stubborn," he teases with the smile that used to melt my heart.

"You're a good neighbor," I say suddenly. "And a good friend. I've missed you."

"Now don't go getting all sappy on me. I'm just a sucker for a damsel in distress."

If he were standing closer, I'd smack him on the shoulder. Instead I just give him a brave smile. He backs up, waves and turns towards his house.

"Hang in there," he says and crunches across my gravel drive. I watch him retreat until he reenters his house.

I look at my tattoo again. It remains silent. "You better be right about this break up," I say, then pull my sleeve down quickly.

After I take out my trash, I feel at loose ends. It's too early to go to work and frankly, I don't know if I will ever work again now that I know most of my clients were faked by my father.

I need to find Aubry, but have no idea where to start. I make a pot of coffee and sit at my kitchen table with a pad of paper and a pink pen. I turn to a blank page and stare at it.

"What do I know so far?" I ask out loud. Chester rubs against my ankle and I reach for him. I pull him onto my lap and bury my face in his fur. My heart still aches and I find it hard to concentrate.

"He'll be okay without us, right?" I say to the cat. He purrs and rubs his chin against mine in response. "And we'll be okay without him. We were alone before."

My throat aches at the thought. Not too long ago, I was alone except for Grandma Dot. I worked at a catalog company as a phone order taker. A job that was not fulfilling, but at least paid the bills. What was I thinking that I could own my own shop and make a living with my gift?

The thought of going back to work at the catalog company makes my stomach turn. I can't see myself sitting at a computer, listening to old ladies trying to decide what color of sheets to buy.

There are bad guys out there. I've stopped some of the worst. River Bend is safer with me out searching for killers.

I pick up my pen and start making notes of all the things I know about Aubry's disappearance.

He's testing me.

He won't hurt her.

I rub my head, trying to remember all the details of the visions I received.

Two people took her – hired help.

She's in an old room. Old house maybe?

There's plenty of old houses around. Many of them abandoned.

Check the abandoned houses.

ries Ke. What does that mean?

Dogs barking.

That could be anything. There are dogs all over River Bend.

I look at my meager list and wonder what I should do next. On impulse, I place my left hand on the list and close my eyes. I wait to see something, even a wisp of something.

I get nothing.

"Aubry, where are you?"

I wonder what work the police have done and wish I could talk to Lucas about the case.

Tears sting my eyes thinking of him.

I'm suddenly exhausted. The horizon is stained pink, but I have a few hours until I need to see my first "client" at the shop. I'd rather be hunting for Aubry, but I don't know where to start or what to do.

I carry Chester to bed and lie down next to him.

I want Lucas to be here. To curl up behind me, one arm under my neck and the other tossed over my waist. My safe place.

"Not anymore," I mutter miserably. Hoping for a dream that will tell me where to find Aubry, I close my eyes.

"Just ten minutes of rest," I say and drift to sleep.

Chapter 18

GABBY

I've barely closed my eyes when there's a hard knock on my front door. Startled, I sit up, disturbing Chester who jumps from the bed. At first, I think it's my father coming back, but quickly realize he'd never knock.

"Gabby! Are you up?" The voice is familiar, but in my sleepy state, I can't place it for a moment. I stumble down the hall to the front door. I check the peek hole and see blond hair.

Lacey Aniston.

I unlock the door and open it.

"Lacey, it's barely morning, what are you doing here?"

"I heard your father escaped from jail and he's behind Aubry's abduction."

"News travels fast," I say, stepping back so she can

come in.

She scans my meager house. Her nose wrinkles, but she refrains from comment.

"Want some coffee?"

"Sure," she follows me into the kitchen and sees my notebook. "Are these notes on Aubry?"

"Yeah. Cream or sugar?" I add a heavy dollop of creamer to my cup.

"Only on Sundays," she says and takes the cup of black coffee. She continues studying the list I made.

"Check out the abandoned houses. We could do that," she says.

"What do you mean we could do that?"

"We have to do something. If your father has her, we have to hurry and find her. Especially after the ransom drop was ruined." I don't miss the undercurrent in the words.

"I saved your dad's life," I remind her.

She shrugs me off. "It made a good story. The poor bridge, though. The fire department stopped it from burning up completely, but it will never be the same."

"I didn't set the bomb." I hate that I feel the need to defend myself. Lacey does that to me.

Silence fills the kitchen and I sip my sweet coffee, wondering if I should bring up the fact that we are sisters. Yesterday, she didn't seem pleased with the news. I search her face, perfectly made up, even though her eyes look tired. If I look hard, I can see a slight resemblance to Nathan McAllister, but honestly, Lacey looks like her mom.

"Stop staring at me. I don't look like him."

I don't ask how she knew what I was thinking. I take another sip of coffee, and look away.

After another beat of silence, she says, "Are you going to change clothes or not?"

I look down at my fuzzy pajama pants and oversized tee. "Change?"

"We have abandoned houses to check. You can't go like that." She barely hides her distaste.

I down the last of my coffee, knowing I'll need all the energy I can get if I have to spend the day with Lacey. "Give me a minute."

"I'll be outside." She fishes her pack of cigarettes from her purse as she goes out the door.

I find a pair of jean shorts that aren't too dirty and one of my favorite tops. I try to get a brush through my hair, but I didn't comb the curls out when they got wet from the river and they are a mess. I put on a little eyeliner.

"You'll never compete with her in that department." Disgusted with myself that I even care what I look like next to Lacey, I toss the pencil into the drawer.

I hurry down the hall, pull on a fresh pair of gloves and my sneakers, then grab the notebook.

I take a deep breath before I open the door. "Wish me luck. Hopefully, I'll bring Aubry home. Or at least manage the day with Lacey," I say to Chester. He licks a paw and ignores me.

I pull open the door and am met with the smell of smoke. Lacey is standing on the steps impatiently. She scans my outfit as I step out, but luckily doesn't comment.

"I'll drive," I say and make my way to the Charger.

She looks like she wants to argue, but concedes and stubs her smoke out on the top step. She looks around for a place to put the butt.

"Trash is at the end of the driveway," I tell her.

She throws the butt away, then climbs in next to me. It seems surreal that Lacey Aniston, my sworn enemy since high school, is sitting next to me in my car.

The engine roars to life and I back out of the driveway.

Lacey looks around. "Cool car," she says.

Surprised at the rare compliment, I say thank you.

"Didn't some guy die in here?" she suddenly says, lifting her legs and looking at the seat below her as if blood will stain her.

"Um, yeah, but I had the car professionally cleaned." She looks under both legs then settles into her seat.

"Where do you want to start?" she asks, apparently satisfied that there isn't blood.

"I thought you knew where we were going?"

"I don't know the back roads the way you do. I rarely leave town."

"I know of a few abandoned properties, I guess we'll start there." I turn towards out of town and we are soon surrounded by corn fields full of baby corn stalks. I love when the corn is tiny and freshly popped from the soil. It feels like hope is growing.

We need hope for this search.

"Are you getting any visions?" she suddenly asks breaking the silence.

"That's not how it works for me. I don't just get visions."

"Dad said you told him you had one at the bridge. I

just hoped maybe you were getting something."

"Are you?"

She squirms in her seat. "No."

"There's an abandoned property just up here," I say searching the stand of woods on our right. "It's hard to see," I peer into the trees and see the red brick of the building peaking through the new leaves on the trees.

I find the weed-choked driveway and pull in. A fallen branch blocks the driveway about half way to the house.

I park the car and look through the windshield towards the crumbling brick house that once was someone's dream home. Now it is covered in vines and small trees are growing from its gutters.

"Doesn't look like anyone is here," Lacey whispers.

"That would be the point, wouldn't it," I point out, not whispering.

"Seems like there would have to be a car or something. Nathan doesn't seem the kind to walk."

I turn off the engine and grab the door handle. "Let's check it out."

Bugs buzz my ears as I climb over the fallen branch. The birds stop singing as we disturb the woods. The quiet is unsettling.

"We'll look through the windows first." I find myself whispering, too.

"Wait," Lacey says as we round the curve of the driveway and the house is in full view before us. "What if she is in there? We know there's at least two of them holding her, plus Nathan."

I feel foolish, I hadn't thought about that. "Good point. We can't just walk up and say, hand her over."

I wish I had a weapon or something. I search the woods and find a branch. I'd rather have a gun and a safety vest like Lucas has, but the stick will have to do.

Lacey looks incredulous. "Is this what you do? Just run in without a plan?"

"This was your idea." I defend myself.

Lacey nibbles on a fingernail, looking around for her own stick. "True. I guess a stick is better than nothing."

"Besides, he said he wouldn't hurt her and I don't think he'd hurt us. We are his daughters."

Her eyes flash and her hair swings wide as she turns on me, "I am not his daughter," she snaps.

"Sorry," I say, opening my arms wide. "I just mean, I don't think he'd hurt us."

"Didn't he once hold you at gunpoint? And he shot

Dustin. We don't know what he's capable of."

I suddenly feel stupid holding the stick, but it's all I have. "Let's just get this over with."

We creep from tree to tree until we reach the house. It feels abandoned, an air of despair hangs over the crumbling pile of bricks.

I crouch below the wide window at the front of the house and slowly raise myself until I can see over the sill.

The house is a mess inside. The wallpaper is peeling and the floor is covered with leaves. I'm pretty sure the place is deserted.

"What a mess," Lacey says next to me.

"It doesn't look like anyone has been here for years."

"Are you getting anything now that we are here?"

I shake my head. "Nothing. Just emptiness and decay."

"Maybe you should touch the door or something."

I certainly don't want to do that. "A place like this is sure to be full of memories. I'd rather not touch it."

"Then let's go in." Before I can stop her, she marches to the front door. I expect it to be locked but it swings open and she disappears inside.

"Lacey, wait."

With the stick firmly in my grasp, I enter the house.

The floor sags under our feet and the stench of decay fills my nose. From upstairs, I hear scurrying and wonder if it's mice or squirrels. Holding our sticks high, we go from room to room.

"Nothing looks disturbed." I motion towards the layer of leaves and dust on the floors. At the back of the house, we find a door hanging wide open. "This must be why there are so many leaves in here. Can you close it?" I ask her. I do not want to touch the handle.

Lacey huffs, but closes the door for me.

We are standing in what looks like the dining room. A closed door is to my left. From behind the door, something crashes.

Chapter 19

GABBY

Lacey turns to me, her eyes huge. "What was that?" she mouths.

I shrug and motion for her to open the door.

She shakes her head.

Something moves behind the door. "Do it." I mouth.

She reaches for the knob that I won't touch and pulls the door open.

A flash of gray flies past us and runs into the back door that we just closed. The blur bounces off the door and shakes its head.

"A raccoon!" Lacey shouts in fear.

The raccoon is stunned for a moment, then turns on us

and hisses.

Lacey hides behind me, squealing.

"It's just a coon," I say, keeping my eye on the angry animal. "He's more afraid of us than we are of him."

"Speak for yourself." She cowers behind me.

"Open the door and he'll go out."

"You open it."

"I can't touch it."

"Well, come with me." Lacey grabs my shoulder and, keeping me between her and the raccoon, and holding her stick at the ready, we shuffle towards the back door.

The coon arches his back and hisses again.

When we are close enough, Lacey turns the knob and throws the door open.

We back away and I raise my stick to scare him out.

Another blur of gray fur and he's gone.

Lacey slumps against my back in relief, then realizing we are touching, she jumps away.

"That was scary," she says.

"We get raccoons in Grandma Dot's barn all the time. They make a smelly mess, but they aren't dangerous unless you corner them."

"I don't want to get rabies."

I try not to laugh. "They won't give you rabies."

"They might." She closes the back door again. "Better to stay away."

I walk through the door the raccoon came out of and scan the kitchen. There are some broken dishes on the floor, obviously knocked over by the coon. "This place is abandoned," I say. "We can check upstairs, but Aubry isn't here."

Lacey drops her stick on the floor. "Let's get out of here."

"Do you know of any more houses we can check?" she asks once we are back in the car.

"I can think of two more, but they are in pretty bad shape. I don't see how he could keep someone in either of them."

"Let's check them out anyway."

I back out of the driveway and head for the next house.

It takes most of the morning. I had appointments this morning, but I skip them. The people my father hired as clients can get stood up. We visit every old house that I can think of. I even call Grandma Dot for leads on others and we check out three more.

We find nothing, not even another raccoon.

We are both tired and frustrated when I pull out of the last driveway. "She has to be somewhere," Lacey says, twisting a length of her hair. She has a smudge of dirt on her cheek and I'm thinking of a way to tell her when my tattoo tingles.

Not now.

I'm suddenly reminded of Lucas and my broken heart. I can't imagine what new bad thing my tattoo will bring me today.

Take the bridge.

I don't have to wonder which bridge. We are only a mile or so from the bridge where Lucas and I had our first kiss. I was trying not to think about it, was going to take a different way home.

With a heavy sigh, I make a left turn and drive towards the bridge.

Lacey is so lost in thought, she doesn't comment on my change of direction.

"There has to be another house somewhere. You saw her in an old house."

I appreciate that she puts so much store in my abilities, but I'm distracted by the message from the tattoo and the bridge that is quickly approaching.

The memory of Lucas's lips on mine and the fact that they may never again touch them swamps me as I pull onto the bridge.

Stop and get out.

Loud and clear.

I want to drive way fast, but I press the brake.

Lacey looks at me in surprise as I put the car into park. "What are you doing?"

I don't know what to tell her, so I climb out of the car and hope no traffic comes.

I look over the side of the bridge into the rushing water below, wondering what I'm supposed to do now that I stopped.

"Gabby, are you okay?" she asks as she gets out of the car and joins me at the railing.

"I thought I heard something," I say lamely.

"A vision?" She exclaims and starts looking around. "Is there something about Aubry here?"

"I don't know."

She suddenly gasps and covers her mouth with her hand. "Oh no. Is that a body?" She points to the bank of the river.

A man lays face down, unmoving.

My heart races. The man is wearing a black long sleeve shirt, just like the men that held Aubry wore last night

"I think it's one of the kidnappers," I say quietly.

Lacey is hurrying down the bridge. "Let's check it out. Maybe he has a clue on him about where Aubry is."

I'm surprised she's not more upset at finding a dead person.

I watch as she climbs down the bank, not following. I don't want to see another dead man. I don't want to touch him and see how he died.

"I don't want to see it, Lord. Don't make me, please," I beg of the breeze.

"Gabby, come on," Lacey calls up to me. "Come touch him."

"We should call the police," I stall.

"We will. But he had Aubry. You might be able to see her or find her or something. I don't know how it works. Just get down here." Her tone leaves no room for argument.

I slowly make my way across the bridge. As I start down the bank, a car crosses the bridge, honking in anger that I'm parked in the lane.

I ignore the car and focus on the man lying half in the water.

"How do you want to do this?" she asks. "Do you need me to turn him over first?"

I don't want to see his face, so I shake my head. "We shouldn't be messing with him at all. This is a crime scene."

"Right, and this is our only chance."

I stall, staring at the man's back and the hole in his shirt that obviously came from a gunshot.

"Please, Gabby. We have to find my sister. *Our* sister." She's pulling all the stops now, laying the guilt on thick.

She's right. If this man was holding Aubry, I might see something useful.

I'll also see his murder. I have no doubt who pulled the trigger causing the bullet hole in his shirt.

My father.

Our father.

He has to be stopped.

"Do it with me. It will give us the best information."

Lacey looks scared but nods.

I take off my glove and kneel next to the body. Lacey kneels beside me and holds the back of my left hand.

"Ready?" I ask. She nods again.

"Lord, let us see what we need to see," I pray and lower my hand.

Chapter 20

GABBY

"Wait," Lacey says and pulls her hand away from mine.

"What," I say exasperated. She practically begged me to do this.

"I don't want to see him die." She looks away across the river. "I don't think I can see that."

I understand. I don't want to see it either. "We need to see what he saw," I explain half-heartedly. "We can see more together than I can see alone."

She picks at an invisible spot on her pants. "I know. I just- I haven't done this before. How do you do it so often?"

"It's not like I enjoy it. But God gave us our gift so we can help others. This is how I help. I need you to help me now." I hold out my bare left hand.

She takes a steadying breath and rests her hand on mine. "Okay. What do we do?"

"Just open your mind." I wrap her fingers in mine and place our hands on the dead man's shoulder.

She looks at me with eyes hooded from the drugs he tells us to give her. Lovely, beautiful. I need to touch her. Skin so soft my fingers are unworthy. Hair like silk. Mine for the taking. If I dare.

Don't touch her.

Caught.

She waits. She's mine.

Pain rips through my shoulder, explodes through my back.

The last thing I see is her staring at me in shock and horror.

She could have been mine.

The vision turns to darkness and I tear my hand away from the man, release Lacey. I feel dirty after the vision, tainted. I rub my hand on my jean shorts but it isn't enough. I climb on my hands and knees to the river's edge and rinse my hands.

"He was going to assault her," Lacey says, shaken.

Tears slide down her cheeks.

"He was," I agree and scrub at my hand.

"He stopped him. He saved her," Lacey is rocking back and forth, her arms wrapped around her knees as she sits in the dirt.

"Maybe he's not a complete monster," I concede. "He still shot the man in cold blood."

"To protect Aubry." She rocks a few times, a soothing rhythm, staring at her hand. "How did we see that? I mean, was it real?"

"It's real," I say, standing. "He's dead isn't he?"

"I mean the rest of it. How do we know what he was thinking?"

"I don't know." I throw my arms out in exasperation. "I just see things, know things. And so do you. I don't know how it works, it just does."

She wipes her hand on her pants. "What do we do now? I don't think we're any closer to finding Aubry."

"At least we know she's still alive." I pace the bank of the river, thinking over the vision. "Did you see anything useful? Like a picture on the wall or anything that would let us know where she is?"

Lacey closes her eyes, running the vision through her

head. "I don't think so. Maybe we should touch him again. Look for details this time."

"Be my guest. I'm not."

I think about the vision, playing every detail in my mind, searching for something I might have missed. "The dogs are still barking," I say.

"I did hear that. But lots of people have dogs."

"Yeah." I run a hand through my curls in frustration. "Crap on a cracker, there has to be something we're not seeing."

I look down at the dead man's back. I should feel sorry for his loss. I should feel sad a fellow human is dead.

But he wanted to assault Aubry. He brought the bullet on himself. It's hard to feel sorry for him.

"Now what?" she asks, standing. "We should call the police, right?"

Lucas is the last person I want to see right now, especially here at our bridge. "Call them."

"Why aren't you doing it? You are dating the detective."

I fight sudden tears, feel my face grow hot. I look away across the river, wishing I was anywhere other than here.

"Oh no," Lacey says, correctly guessing my dilemma.

"He broke up with you, didn't he?"

"No," I protest, wiping at my eyes. "I broke up with him."

Lacey tosses her hair over her shoulder. "You're dumber than I thought you were. He's a catch." She pulls her phone from her pocket and dials 911.

I start up the bank, ready to go. "You can't leave me here alone with a dead body," Lacey calls after me, then talks to the dispatcher that answered. "Yes, this is Lacey Aniston," she says.

I don't hear the rest of her conversation. I climb into the Charger, ready to drive away to anywhere. But she's right. I can't leave her here alone.

A car passes, slowing to a crawl. I wave it on.

"At least get off the bridge and out of traffic," I grumble and pull the car off the bridge and to the side of the road.

I sit in the car, watch Lacey struggle her way up the bank. She approaches my open window. "They are on the way."

"Great. Soon as they get here, I'm leaving."

She stands outside my door. "Sorry about calling you stupid," she says.

I grip the steering wheel. "That's okay. I don't understand it myself."

"Then why did you do it?"

I am not about to tell Lacey about the tattoo and the messages. "I just had to, that's all."

She's twisting her hair again. "Okay. Fair enough." We wait in silence for a few moments. "We are going to find her, right?"

"Of course. I just don't know how yet." I wish I was as sure as I sounded.

I suddenly realize I'm starving. Visions do that to me. I dig through the center console until I find the bag of caramels I keep there. "Want one?" I offer.

She shakes her head, "No, but can you hand me my purse?" She digs inside until she finds her cigarettes and lighter. She lights one and takes a deep drag. Some of the tension leaves her shoulders.

"Is it always like that?" she asks, motioning to the dead man.

"Like what?"

"Fade to black. Do you think death is really like that?"

"It usually is like that. I can't see what happens after they leave here."

"You think there is an afterlife? Something to be seen?"

"I do."

"Do you see ghosts?"

"I've seen a few strange things, but I don't think I've seen a ghost. I do believe they can exist, though."

She takes another long drag and blows it away from my window.

"Do you think he loved her?" she asks out of the blue.

"Nathan and your mom?"

"Yes." She looks away.

"He told me last night that he's always loved her. That's why he's doing this. To get back at your dad."

The tension returns to her shoulders. "So Aubry has to suffer?"

"He doesn't think like that. He's a sociopath. He only cares about what's good for him."

"But he's your dad."

"He ceased being my dad the night he left me for dead," I rub at the scar on my eyebrow, "And framed my mom for his murder."

"Is that why you call him Nathan?"

"It's better than the four letter words I'd rather call

him," I break into a smile.

Lacey laughs. "You're not half bad, Gabby." She says. "I should have been nicer to you."

That's an understatement, but I let it slide. "You, too."

The sound of a car approaching intrudes on our nice moment. I recognize the shape behind the wheel. "The cavalry is here." I start the Charger's engine.

"You're really going to leave me here?"

"Lucas and Dustin will give you a ride back to town."

"My car is at your house," she sounds like she really doesn't want me to leave.

"Then that's where they'll take you. Tell them what we saw."

"I can't do that," she protests. "I don't want them to know about that part of me."

"Then tell them what I saw. Give as many details as possible."

"Why don't you do it?"

Lucas parks his car next to mine and Dustin climbs out of the passenger seat. Lucas looks straight ahead, avoiding looking my way.

"Please, I need to leave." I feel like I can't breathe. I put the car in reverse and check my mirrors. "You can do this."

Lucas is climbing out of the car. I have to get away.

I leave Lacey with the men and pull onto the road. When I check my rear view mirror, I see the man I love watching me drive away.

I burst into tears. "Why?!" I scream at God. "I need him!"

Every part of me wants to turn around, tell him I made a mistake.

Keep driving.

I rub my arm violently, hating the tattoo and what it says. If I had a knife, I'd cut it out of my skin right now. That wouldn't stop the messages.

The afternoon sun is bright on the fields. I check the time. If I hurry, I can still make one of my appointments. Maybe it's a real customer, not a fake sent by Nathan.

I think of my mortgage and the overhead at the shop. Fake or not, I could use the money.

And the distraction.

I park next to Mom's white car in the alley and let myself into the shop. I have ten minutes to spare. I go to the front door and unlock it. I check the traffic on the square and see a familiar car on the far side.

Alexis.

"Why is she always over there?" I ask the empty room and walk onto the sidewalk. I hurry across the square to her car, looking at every face, searching for my sister in law. When I don't see her, I search all the doors. There's a restaurant on the corner, but she's not in it. A real estate office is empty as well. The only other door near her car is for a church.

This isn't the church her and Dustin go to.

I approach the glass door, put my hands around my face to block the sun, and peer in.

Inside is just an open room, with some people sitting at the far end, barely visible from the street.

I can't see much, so I open the door and enter.

A man is standing, talking to the group. At first, I think he's the preacher giving a sermon. I search the heads watching him for Alexis. One of the women looks like her, but I can't be sure from the view of the back of her head.

The man stops talking and looks at me. "Come in, come in. Join us. Don't be shy." His welcome is warm. I take a few steps towards the group. The woman I thought was Alexis turns her head. It's her. And her mouth falls open in shock when she sees me.

"Gabby, what in the world are you doing here?" she exclaims, her face flaming crimson.

"Alexis, what's going on?"

She hurries from her seat and shuffles me towards the door. "I'm sorry," she says to the group, then pulls me outside.

"What's going on?" I demand. "I've seen you over here before."

She looks across the town square, tucks a stray strand of hair behind her ear. "You wouldn't understand."

"Try me," I say.

"This is an AA meeting." She meets my eyes, daring me to look away.

"Alcoholics Anonymous? That's what this is about?"

She breaks the eye contact and tucks her hair again. "I've been coming for several months. You can't tell Dustin. He doesn't know."

"You can't keep this from him. If you have a problem, he needs to know."

"No he doesn't. This is my business and my issue. He has enough to worry about." She grabs my arm, pleading.

"Gabby, you can't tell."

I'm shocked that she is touching me. She barely talks to me, let alone touch me. "Okay, okay. I won't tell him, but you need to. Wait, where's Walker?"

She looks at the ground. "Grandma Dot is watching him."

"She knows?"

"Yes. She's been helping me get better. I am getting better. I'm ninety days sober."

"That's wonderful," I say with honest approval. "The meetings must be helping."

"They are." She looks towards the door. "I should be getting back in there."

"Of course."

Alexis surprises me again by throwing her arms around me for a quick hug, our first since her wedding.

"It's hard, you know. Being married to a cop."

"I imagine it is."

"You should think about that before you get too far with Lucas."

His name hits me like a punch to the gut. She's gone back into the meeting before I can respond with, "I don't need to worry about that anymore.

Chapter 21

DUSTIN

When Lucas wakes me up to tell me my father has escaped from jail, I know my day is going to be a bad one.

Alexis is curled in a tight ball on her side of the bed. I long to reach for her, to touch her hip. I can tell by her breathing she is awake, but she doesn't roll over to talk to me like she used to when I got called out.

"My father showed up at Gabby's tonight," I tell her.

She shifts slightly but doesn't face me. "I thought he was in jail."

"He was. He apparently escaped."

"Good luck," she says to the wall.

I climb out of bed, pull on the first pair of pants I find and leave her.

For the life of me, I don't understand what has changed

with us. The paranoid part of me thinks maybe she's seeing someone. Maybe she wants out and doesn't know how to tell me.

The scared part of me thinks if I just give her space, she'll come back to me and we will be close like we used to be.

I close the bedroom door behind me and go to check on Walker.

He's asleep on his side, rolled into a tight ball like his mother. I don't hesitate to touch him and place my hand on his precious head. I've barely been home lately and miss him.

He stirs under my touch and I pull my hand away. Alexis will be angry if I wake him right as I'm leaving. I back to the door and he settles back to sleep, one pudgy hand curled under his cheek. I blow him a silent kiss and head out into the night to my sister.

Lucas is already at her house when I arrive. I'm surprised to see him in uniform, and wish that I had put something else on besides the pajama pants I found on the floor. Gabby is waiting on her front step.

We go over what Nathan McAllister said to her, what we need to know. Then the conversation turns awful.

She's crying and saying words I never thought I'd hear her say. "We're over."

My best friend and partner is visibly shaken. I wish I was anywhere other than witnessing the end of their relationship.

I toe the sidewalk and try to make myself invisible. "You're unbelievable," I tell her then drive away.

In the car, I can't believe what I just witnessed. Gabby may have her issues, she even believes God talks to her. I never thought she'd hurt Lucas like that. I catch up to his cruiser and follow him to the station.

I push thoughts of Gabby and Lucas and their relationship out of my mind. We have work to do.

Nathan McAllister is loose and has a girl held hostage.

I change at the station into a spare uniform I keep in my locker and get to work.

After a long and fruitless morning, the last thing we expect is the call that comes into dispatch. We are sitting at our desks, discussing what our next steps should be when the call comes in.

"Lacey Aniston called to report a dead body washed up in the river."

"Where at?" I ask, standing.

They give the address and Lucas pales. I know that bridge is close to his father's house.

"I'm sure Gregor is fine," I say.

"I'm not worried about that," he says, brushing off my concern. "Let's just go. At least Gabby didn't find the body this time."

We were wrong about that. Her car is parked on the far side of the bridge. Lacey is standing next to the driver's side door.

"What are those two doing together way out here?" I ask.

Lucas grips the steering wheel tighter and keeps his eyes straight ahead, avoiding the Charger.

"I don't care," he grumbles.

I climb out first, ready to grill Gabby, but she pulls out and drives away.

"What got into her?" I ask Lacey.

She shrugs. "Who knows. She just said she had to go."

Lucas watches the car drive away and then turns his attention to the crime scene. "Where is he?"

"Down there," Lacey says and points to a man face down at the side of the river.

"How in the world did you two even see him way out here?" I ask.

"Gabby just drove here, then stopped the car and got out. She's a bit erratic, you know."

Lucas makes a sound of derision. "You could say that."

"Sorry to hear about you two," Lacey says gently.

"I'm not," he grumbles back and begins down the bank.

"Did she, you know, touch him before she left?" I ask Lacey.

"She did. He's one of the men holding my sister. He was going to assault Aubry. He wanted her. Then your dad stopped him. The next thing we knew, he was shot. Nathan must have dumped him here."

I hear the "we" but let it go.

"Or upriver," I say looking in that direction. "The current here is pretty strong. He could have been thrown in anywhere that way."

"I suppose so," she says thoughtfully, twirling her hair. "Look, can I get a ride out of here? Your sister just left me and my car is at her house."

I want to ask why they are together, but knowing

Gabby I won't like the answer. "Dustin," Lucas calls before I can form the words. "He's been shot. There's a nasty exit wound on his back."

"Yeah, he's one of Nathan's men holding Aubry. Apparently, he tried something on her and was shot because of it."

Lucas stares at me from down the bank. "And you know this how?"

I point in the direction Gabby drove off in.

"Why even be detectives if she's just going to swoop in and figure things out without us?" He turns his anger on Lacey. "Let me guess, she touched the body? A fresh crime scene and she's down here mucking it up."

Lacey's mouth opens for a sharp retort. I touch her shoulder to stop her. "He's having a bad day. Let it go."

Her mouth snaps shut.

"We will get you a ride back as soon as we can. Maybe a patrol officer can take you. It might be a while. You can sit in the cruiser if you want."

Lacey tosses her hair and goes to sit in the passenger seat of the cruiser.

I climb down the bank to the body. Lucas has on gloves and is checking the man's pockets for an ID. I know he won't find one. Nathan would never be that careless.

"His pockets are empty," he says.

We both look as the sound of a car approaches. "Coroner Gomez is here," I say.

"Great," he says sarcastically. "I'll get blamed for Gabby being here and messing with the body."

"We don't have to tell her."

"But we know this man's identity, well sort of. We can't keep that secret."

"We're the detectives. It's our business what we know and what we share."

"So Gabby was never here?"

"Exactly."

"How do we explain Lacey being here and finding the body?" he asks.

"She was out jogging. She was so upset about her sister, she needed to blow off some steam so she went for a long run. A woman like that probably runs all the time."

He looks thoughtful, for a moment, then agrees.

"Gabby was never here and Gomez won't have a reason to chew my butt."

"That's the story."

He looks at the body of the man. "Probably shot in the shoulder, based on the exit wound. Thank God his aim was worse when he shot you."

I rub the spot where my father shot me, and stretch the shoulder that aches most of the time.

"Thank God," I agree.

"Stand back, detectives," Gomez shouts down at us from the bridge. "Don't contaminate the scene."

We both step back from the man and let Gomez take over.

Chapter 22

GABBY

I make it back to the shop as my client is arriving. They are carrying something wrapped in a brown paper bag. The woman holds it tight to her chest. I search her face and she seems genuinely concerned with what she's brought for me to touch. Either she's a great actress or not one of Nathan's fakes.

I spend the next half hour with the woman and her grandma's antique jewelry box. I tell her the history of the box and the contents. Luckily the memories are happy ones. I don't think I could take any more negative energy flowing through me today.

The woman thanks me profusely as she leaves. The familiar pride in my work fills me. I helped this woman, I made a difference. She appreciates my gift.

I watch her walk down the sidewalk and get into her

car.

"You did good," Mom says from the stairs, startling me.

I spin around. "How long have you been there?"

"I came down right as she was arriving. I didn't want to bother you." She descends the last of the steps. "You really are quite remarkable, you know."

"Tell that to Lucas," I grumble, my heart aching as I flop down on yellow couch where the woman sat a moment ago.

"That boy loves you." Mom sits next to me.

I rub my face, will the tears not to come. "We broke up," I manage.

"Oh no, Gabby." Mom's arms are around me in an instant and I melt into her. "What happened?"

I'd have to tell her about the tattoo and it's messages for her to understand. I hesitate, then dive in.

I pull up my sleeve and explain how God talks to me, hoping she won't pull away in disgust or fear.

She wraps her arm around my shoulder and holds me tighter. "Even more remarkable. No wonder Nathan wants you to join him in his criminal pursuits. Of course, if he knew God talked to you, maybe he'd realize you'd never help him do evil."

I sniff and sit up straight. "He does know." I explain about the fake clients and how he's been studying me.

"I heard he was at your house last night. How that man can keep conning everyone is beyond me. Of course, I married him so that makes me the biggest fool."

"He wasn't always like this," I say. "I remember him being very different when we were kids."

Mom rubs her hands down her thighs, a nervous habit. "I suppose he was different then. I just don't know what made him change."

"Greed will do that to the best of us," I point out. "I feel sorry for him, really. He's a miserable man trying to control everything and everyone around him."

Mom makes a sound of disgust. "Don't feel sorry for him. He's brought all the bad on himself."

"Don't worry. He's on my number one enemy list. Right now, I need to find Aubry. If this is all a test, I must pass it. For her sake."

"He said this was all a test for you?"

I nod my head, "Yep. And so was the bridge he blew up last night."

She shakes her head in disgust. "He really is sick. So

what are you going to do?"

I tell her about searching the abandoned houses. "I don't know where to go now." A yawn cuts through me, so large it hurts my jaw.

Mom pats my hand. "Looks like you could use some rest."

"I can't. Aubry is counting on me." Another yawn takes hold.

"Have you eaten yet today?" Mom asks.

"No, just some candy."

She stands and pulls on my hand. "Come on. Your grandma is making lasagna tonight. That's where I was headed when I came down the steps."

My mouth waters thinking of Grandma Dot's lasagna and my stomach growls loudly.

"Guess a girl's gotta eat."

After soothing my tired soul by listening to some Twenty One Pilots and singing along like a wild person, I park near the barn at Grandma Dot's. Mom parks next to me and finds me chuckling at the memory of the raccoon that scared Lacey and me.

"Those coons are terrifying," she says pointing to the

barn. "When I was a kid, one chased me out of the hay loft."

It feels good to laugh a little. "I haven't been in that barn for years. I wonder if there's any in there now?" She muses.

The large bank barn looms. The sliding door on the side is hanging open, Grandma's Kubota tractor is parked just inside. "Looks like Grandma was out tilling today," I say and walk over to close the door. It takes both Mom and me to pull the heavy wooden door along its track.

"The track must need greased," Mom says. "I wonder if Mr. Sickmiller still does that kind of thing for her?"

Last time I saw Mr. Sickmiller, he was on the side of the road. He was in no shape to be climbing ladders with a grease gun. "Knowing Grandma, she'll be out here on a ladder before the day ends."

We both giggle at that and climb the steps to the porch and let ourselves into the kitchen.

"Grandma, you're being invaded," I call. The kitchen smells wonderfully of garlic and baking tomatoes. My stomach growls again. Jet bounds across the floor to meet us and I pick him up.

"Gabriella, you came," Grandma Dot says as she

enters the kitchen.

"I heard there was lasagna. Of course I came right over."

Grandma puts on her chicken print hot pads and takes the lasagna from the oven. "You're just in time. I made an extra large one. Pauline is coming for dinner and I figured you'd be here at some point."

"How is Mrs. Mott?" Mom asks. "I've barely seen her lately."

"She has a new man," Grandma says in a whisper. "He's younger than her."

I warm to the gossip, "How much younger?" I whisper back.

"Fifteen years. Of course, she and I need a younger man to keep up with us."

"Of course," I giggle, the tension leaving my shoulders. Jet wriggles in my lap.

Grandma grows serious and looks me in the eye, the steam from the lasagna floating between us. "I heard about your father and what he's doing to you."

I don't ask how she knows. All the news in River Bend comes through Grandma's beauty shop at some point.

"It was quite a shock finding him in my bedroom last

night."

Grandma scrunches her face in disgust. "Would it kill him to ring the bell like a normal person? No he has to sneak into your room."

"And out of jail," I say.

Grandma tosses the hot pad on the counter. "We need a better jail if they are just going to let the likes of Nathan escape. At least you are okay. I saw on the news that the bridge exploded last night. Lacey left your name out of it, but Alexis told me all about what she heard from Dustin." She suddenly snaps her mouth shut at mention of Alexis.

I let it slide, not wanting her to know I am aware that she's been watching Walker while Alexis goes to Alcoholics Anonymous meetings. It's not my story to talk about.

"Yeah," I say with faked casualness. "I might have had to jump into the river with Anthony Aniston."

Mom gasps. "I didn't know you were there. Oh my, Gabby."

I shrug off her concern. "No worries. Nathan said he had no intention of me getting hurt. He just wanted me to think I might. It was another test."

"Oh, that man!" Grandma exclaims. "If I ever get my

hands on him." She makes a gesture of choking someone.

"He's no match for you," I say, giggling again.

Grandma takes plates out of the cabinet and Mom gets out glasses. I soak up the simple moment from my seat at the kitchen bar.

Grandma feels me watching her and turns slowly, the plates held in mid-air. She studies my face and gets a faraway look in her eyes. "You're different. I can sense something."

Grandma likes to think she has a touch of the psychic powers, too. I've always thought she was just good at reading people.

My face burns. "Nothing's different," I lie.

"She and Lucas broke up," Mom says quietly.

Grandma slams the plates on the counter. "He broke up with you? How dare he?"

"I appreciate the support, but I broke up with him."

"Gabriella, why? You love him."

I can't meet her eyes, so focus on Jet and rub him behind the ears. "My tattoo told me to. It was very clear about it."

She loses her defensive posture and simply says, "Oh."

I'm glad I don't have to explain to her, she just

understands the importance.

"Well, I suppose that's that then," she says, opening a drawer and taking out a large knife.

"I suppose," I concede. I'd hoped she'd tell me I had been wrong, that I need to fight to get him back.

"You drinking tea?" Mom asks, pointedly changing the subject. Normally, Grandma's tea fixes everything. Tonight I want something stronger.

"You got any wine?"

Grandma snaps her fingers in the air. "Wine. Good idea. Emily, I think there's a bottle or two in that cabinet over there."

Mom retrieves a bottle of pink moscato and pours us each a glass. I set Jet on the floor and stand up from my stool.

"To new beginnings," Grandma says, clinks our glasses and takes a sip. "Um, that's good."

I take a large swig from my glass, enjoying the bite of the sweet liquid. I'm not much of a drinker, but tonight it seems right.

We stand in the kitchen in silence, each of us sipping, the lasagna steaming between us.

"So how are we going to find Aubry?" Grandma

suddenly breaks the silence.

I take another large swig of wine before I answer. The alcohol buzzes my brain slightly and I relish the rush. "I have no earthly idea," I say, then finish my glass.

"You won't do it in earthly ways," Grandma says. "You have to do it your way."

"Fill my glass and I'll show you what I got so far." I leave the kitchen and retrieve the notebook from my car. I'm a little unsteady, my low tolerance from never drinking alcohol making the wine work fast.

I'd left my phone in the car and see I missed a text from Lacey.

"Done at the crime scene and back to get my car. You are not home? Where are you?"

I text her back. "Grandma Dot's," and slip the phone into my pocket.

The shadow of the barn envelopes me. My head buzzes slightly. I stare up at the evening sky, listening. "Where are you, Aubry?"

The door of the barn creaks as the wind blows against it. The new spring leaves on the large trees nearby rustle, sounding like bones rattling. A bug buzzes past my ear. In the distance a dog barks.

All the sounds of the country, nothing to lead me to Aubry.

My phone beeps in my pocket. "Be right there." A text from Lacey. I hadn't meant my text to be an invitation, but Lacey did.

Mrs. Mott's car pulls in as I make my way up the porch steps. Good thing Grandma made a big lasagna.

Chapter 23
GABBY

I toss the notebook on the kitchen island and say, "Mrs. Mott is here."

"Great. We can eat now." Grandma carries the lasagna to the table as Jet starts barking at the back door.

"Hush, Jet, it's just me," Mrs. Mott says as she blows into the kitchen. She pats at a stray hair on her light purple poof. "Phew. Thought I would never get here. Derek and I were in Fort Wayne earlier. We went to the mall and the lines were crazy. I had to wait for two people ahead of me. You don't get lines like that in River Bend."

I smile. Mrs. Mott is always excited about something.

"Yes we do, Pauline. You just want to complain," Grandma teases.

"Well, maybe," she concedes. "At least the company was good." She looks at me. "Did she tell you I have a new beau?"

"She did. A much younger man."

"Indeed," she pats her hair again. "You should see what I bought at Victoria's Secret today. He picked it out."

"Mrs. Mott," I admonish and take a sip of my wine.

"What?" she feigns innocence. "I may be old, but I'm not dead."

"That's enough of that talk," Grandma says. "Time to eat."

"I almost forgot. Lacey texted and asked where I was. She invited herself over."

"In that case we'll wait." She takes the last sip of her wine. "We are having wine with dinner tonight," she tells Mrs. Mott. "Very European."

"I'd love some." Mrs. Mott helps herself to the last of the bottle. "Gabby, I heard you are knee deep in the missing Aniston girl case. Even blew up a bridge and ruined the ransom drop."

"That's not how it happened," I try to explain.

"Very exciting. I don't know how you do it?"

"I just do what I need to do."

"And how's that handsome detective of yours? Off solving the case?"

The room grows quiet. Mom clears her throat.

"He's not mine anymore."

"Oh," she says simply, then lifts her glass. "Well, here's to the single life."

I drink to that.

We chat a few moments until Lacey pulls into the driveway. I watch her out the back windows as she climbs the porch steps. She looks tired and worried. I feel bad for her. We've come a long way from our previous relationship of sworn enemies.

Lacey knocks primly on the kitchen door. Jet barks at the sound.

Mom opens the door, quieting Jet. "Hi, Lacey. Come on in."

Lacey Aniston is standing in Grandma's kitchen. If you'd asked me last week if that was possible, I would have said no way.

"Come on in and sit down. We are having wine. Would you like some?" Grandma Dot says.

Lacey looks at me, uncertain. I show her my glass. "I

suppose a little won't hurt."

"I'll open the other bottle," Mom says, reaching into the cabinet.

Lacey looks unsure of herself and a little scared. I'm not used to seeing her like that. It makes me like her more, to be honest.

"How you holding up?" Grandma asks.

"I'm hanging in there. I'll feel a lot better once Aubry is home, regardless of Nathan's promise not to hurt her. He did protect her from that dead man."

"Dead man?" Mom asks. "You didn't tell me about that," she scolds me.

"I've had a lot going on today. Besides, I can't talk about open cases."

Grandma presses her lips together in displeasure, then says, "That never stopped you before. Did you two find him?"

"Yes. It was the strangest thing. Gabby drove to a bridge then just stopped and there he was," Lacey says. I wish she'd stop talking.

Grandma gives me a knowing look. "Just stopped, huh?"

I put my hand over my tattoo, wanting to hide it and

what it means.

"You sure know how to find trouble," Mom says shaking her head.

"That's our girl," Mrs. Mott says and raises her glass as if in toast.

Lacey watches the whole exchange with interest. "You're all a tad nuts, aren't you?"

"You bet," Mrs. Mott says and takes another sip.

"Can we just eat?" I ask and take my seat at the table. "Here, Lacey, you can have Dustin's seat." I push the chair out with my foot. Everyone else joins us.

Lacey sits down gingerly. "The lasagna smells delicious," she comments.

Grandma scoops into it and gives Lacey a large helping. "Dig in."

We all enjoy the meal as Mrs. Mott entertains us with stories of her and her new boyfriend, Derek's, latest adventures.

Lacey doesn't say anything during the meal, but shoots me some covert looks. She has something on her mind.

After we finish eating, she finally says something. "I think I'll step outside. Gabby, will you join me?"

She takes her cigarette pack from her purse. I know

there's more coming than an after dinner smoke.

Once we are on the porch, she lights up and remains quiet.

"What's on your mind? Do you have a new lead or an idea of what we should do next?"

She inhales then blows smoke before she answers. "Sort of."

I grow excited. "What is it?"

"It's a little out there, but we're desperate." She inhales again. "I don't know if I want to share my secret with your family."

"They've been nothing but supportive of me having the gift. Even Mrs. Mott. I'm sure they will be supportive of yours, too."

"Do you believe we have the same blood? The same DNA?"

That catches me off guard. "I have to. That's what the test showed."

"Then let's try it. You're not afraid of knives are you?"

She stubs out her smoke and holds the door for me.

"I mean, I guess everyone is. What do you have in mind?"

"A sort of ceremony. A way to reach Aubry. Kind of

like we did in her room, but with blood."

"Blood?" I say as I enter the kitchen. Everyone turns at the word.

"If we have the same blood and so does Aubry, let's see if we can use the blood to reach her." She turns to face the room of questioning faces and lifts her chin. "You all know Gabby has a gift. Well, so do I. It's not as strong as hers, but it can help us see."

No one says anything for a beat.

"That's wonderful," Grandma Dot says.

"How interesting," Mom adds.

"Especially with you two being half sisters," Mrs. Mott chimes in.

"You mentioned blood?" I prompt

"Dot, can we use your sharpest knife?"

I don't like where this is going, but will do what I need to.

Lacey takes my hand and pulls me towards the sink. Grandma removes a knife from a block on the counter.

"What are you going to do with it?" she asks.

Lacey ignores the question and runs the knife across her palm. Blood drips from her hand into the sink. She gives me the knife. "Your turn."

I take off my gloves and touch my left palm with the knife tip. My palm is scarred from where it was once burned. This should be easy compared to that.

"Do it," she demands.

I press the tip of the blade into my skin until it bleeds, then draw it across the scar.

She grabs my hand and presses her bloody palm against mine.

A sizzle tingles up my arm. "Now, do what you do."

I hold onto the counter with my other hand and close my eyes. "Lord, let me see what I need to see."

I entwine my fingers with Lacey's and squeeze the bloody palms together. I focus all my mental power on the blood, similar blood to Aubry's.

"Where are you?" I ask the universe the same way I did earlier.

This time I see something. A window with cracked glass. My sight is blurry. At first I think it's the wine, then I realize it's Aubry and the drugs they've given her.

I focus on the wall by the window, the blue wallpaper is peeling, but I can't see any other helpful details.

I turn my focus to the view from the window.

I see part of a sign. The letters "ries Ke" are visible

between tree branches. I hear dogs barking. Then footsteps behind me.

"Where'd you go?" It's Nathan's voice. "You look really out of it. Drummond, how much of that did you give her?"

"Just what you told me," a man answers.

"Why does she look so out of it? Hey? Come back." Nathan slaps Aubry and the vision disappears.

Lacey collapses against the sink and lets go of my hand.

"We saw her. We really saw her," she says. "It worked."

"What did you see?" Grandma asks.

"Not much," I say, trying to catch my breath. "Part of a sign. The same sign we saw before."

"What did it say?" Mom asks.

"Just parts of words. I have no idea what it means."

"What were the letters?" Mom asks handing Lacey and me paper towels to clean up the blood.

After I wrap my hand in the paper towel, I flip the notebook on the kitchen island open. "These letters." I point to where I wrote them this morning.

Everyone looks at the notebook.

"Were they kind of curly? Like a fancy font?" Mrs. Mott asks.

"They were," I say surprised. "Do you know what they mean?"

She picks up a pen and adds letters to what I wrote.

Von Aries Kennels.

"That's the sign out on Brenton Rd."

I squeeze the paper towel against the pain in my hand. "Are you sure?"

"I mean, it fits the letters," she says.

"But she's not at a kennel. She's in an old house," Lacey says. "We have seen the house."

I look to Mrs. Mott, hoping she can enlighten us further. She shrugs and says, "I don't know anything about an abandoned house, but I've seen the sign."

"We have to go," Lacey says. "She has to be there. We heard the dogs, remember." She is gathering up her purse, ready to run out after Aubry.

"Wait. You can't just go after Nathan like that. You might get hurt," Grandma Dot says.

"We won't go after him," I say. "We're just going to look around a bit and if we find something we'll call Dustin."

"Promise?" Mom asks.

I don't want to make a promise I might not keep, so I don't answer.

"Let's go," Lacey says, grabbing my arm with her paper towel wrapped hand.

"At least let me bandage your cuts," Grandma says, taking a first aid kit out of a cabinet.

We allow her to dry our wounds and put on bandaids, each of us impatient to get on the road.

"You promise you won't do anything stupid?" Mom tries again.

I kiss her on the cheek. "Go home and don't worry. I've done worse before."

"That doesn't bring me comfort," she says.

I give Grandma a quick good-bye hug and thank Mrs. Mott for the tip, then join Lacey who's already outside.

"I'll drive," she says. "I need to smoke."

I don't argue. I just climb into the passenger seat, hoping we're not making a mistake.

Chapter 24

GABBY

When Lacey said she needed to smoke, she wasn't kidding. She lights a cigarette as soon as we are in the car. I run my window down and push my hand against the force of the wind like I did as a kid.

"Sorry," she says. "I really don't normally smoke this much. Just nervous."

"I get it. I normally don't drink. Been a rough few days," I make a sound of derision.

"Just a bit," she answers sarcastically. She takes a drag, thinking. I run my hand up and down against the wind, loving the feel of it on my palm.

I suddenly realize I'm not wearing gloves.

"Crap on cracker." I pull my hand into the car and look around me like a pair of gloves are going to appear on her floor board.

"What's wrong?"

"I left my gloves back at Grandma's. You don't happen to have any in here?"

"It's April. I don't wear gloves in April."

I ball my hands into fists as if that will help.

"Do you want me to go back?"

I think of Aubry alone and drugged with Nathan and the mysterious Drummond. Every minute she is there, she is in danger. "No. I'll be okay." I place my balled hands in my lap.

"You really think those help you?"

"They help. I've been wearing them since high school."

She suddenly laughs, "Yeah. I remember making fun of you for it."

My face burns with the memory. I was not popular in school and Lacey was head cheerleader. We couldn't have been more different.

"I remember that, too."

"I suppose I should say sorry for that."

"That's an odd apology."

"Come on, you did bring it on yourself to some degree," she says and the Lacey I'm used to is back.

"Imagine having the gift I do and trying to learn to deal with it at the same time I was learning to grow up. It wasn't easy."

She grows serious, "Yeah. It wasn't. Hiding who you really are from everyone. At least people knew about you. I've had to keep the secret."

"I just got my house vandalized and made fun of when I went to the store," I add slyly. Not long ago, Lacey terrorized me about my gift in the superstore in town.

"I suppose I should apologize for that, too."

"I wouldn't want you to hurt yourself," I tease and bump her on the shoulder with my balled-up hand.

"No, really. I'm sorry," she says seriously.

"Don't worry about it. I've had worse from lots of people." I settle back in my seat, feeling good. Is this what it's like to have a sister? Dustin and I never tease like this. We just fight.

We turn onto Brenton Rd. "Mrs. Mott said the sign is just up ahead," I say. "Slow down and let's see what we find."

"What are we going to do if we find the house?" she

asks worriedly.

"I don't know." I scan the woods surrounding us, looking for the sign or the house. "We could call Dustin first, I suppose."

"Or be sure she's there first. I don't want to have to explain to him about what we did unless we have to." She holds up her bandaged hand.

"Good point." I scan the road ahead. "There's the sign."

As it was in the vision, the Von Aries Kennels sign has letters that curl at the ends, some fancy font.

Lacey slows the car to a crawl. "Now what?" she whispers.

I scan the woods behind the sign and see the kennels down a lane. "We know she's not at the kennel, just somewhere where she can see the sign. Stop the car."

I climb out onto the quiet country road. We are far from River Bend and haven't seen a car since we turned on Brenton Rd. The surrounding woods are beginning to sing with the evening bugs and frogs. It's an eerie sound. The sun is dipping low behind us.

"Kind of creepy out here," Lacey says, joining me. She slaps at a mosquito on her arm. "Stupid bugs."

I walk to the sign. "If she can see this, we should be able to see her." I put my back to the sign, my head in front of the "ries Ke" part of the sign. I look into the woods behind the sign and only see trees in the fading light. "There's nothing back there."

I go to the other side of the sign and do the same thing. This view looks across the road into another stand of trees.

Between the branches I catch a glimpse of white siding. "It's there!"

Lacey lines her head up with the sign and looks, too. "Holy crap, it really is. It worked."

She starts across the road.

"Wait," I call.

"Aubry is there. You call your brother if you want, I'm going to get her."

She finds an overgrown path that used to be a driveway and starts into the woods. A few paces in, she stops and turns to me. "You coming?"

I feel for my phone in my pocket, but it isn't there. "I don't have my phone." I return to the car and check the floor, hoping it fell out. The corner of my pink phone case peeks out from between the seat and the center console.

By the time I fish it out, Lacey has disappeared up the lane.

I tuck the phone back into my pocket, shoving it low so it won't fall out, and hurry down the lane to catch up to her.

I find her crouching behind a tree at the end of the driveway, a thick stick in her hand. I find my own stick and join her. "You see anything?" I whisper.

She shakes her head. The house before us is practically covered in vines. White siding shows in a few patches, but it's almost camouflaged in the fading light, a perfect hide-out.

There are two windows on the front of the house. One is covered in vines, the other has been cleared. The window Aubry was looking out.

I turn my head towards the sign and can see a part of it.

"She has to be there," Lacey says. "Can you feel her?"

I listen to the universe, and even touch my tattoo, but I get nothing.

A light suddenly flickers into life inside the room. Someone lit a candle.

Lacey looks at me. "Let's go."

I pull on her arm to keep her hidden. "What are you

going to do? Knock on the door and ask for her?"

"You won the contest. You found her. He has to give her up."

"This isn't a game. He won't just hand her over. He still wants his money. Plus, he killed a man recently, remember."

She looks at our sticks, poor weapons against his gun. "What do we do?"

"We need a plan." I chew on my lower lip, thinking, wishing my tattoo would tingle with some ideas.

"Maybe he's not in there," she offers half-heartedly. A shadow passes between the candle and the window.

"Someone is."

I smack at a mosquito buzzing my ear. We can't just sit here, so close but not helping. "I'm calling Dustin." I fish my phone out of my pocket and dial his number.

It takes three rings until he answers. "What?"

"Be nice. You're going to want to hear what I have to say."

"I doubt it."

"We found Aubry. At least we found a house where we think they are holding her. We haven't actually seen her in there yet."

He is all ears now. "You are there now? What's the address?" I tell him about the kennel. "I know the place."

"What should we do?"

"You should find a safe place and wait for us to handle it."

"But she's right there. What if he's hurting her?"

"If you used some of your gift to find her then you also know if she's being hurt. Is she?"

"Not that I know of," I concede.

"Then you can wait a few minutes until we get there. I'll have to call S.W.A.T. to do the takedown. Please, Gabby for once in your life let the police handle this."

He's right and I know it. "Okay," I say. "But hurry."

"We always hurry." He hangs up.

Lacey is staring at me. "We're supposed to just wait for him aren't we?"

"We should go back to the car."

"But we're so close," she protests.

I don't wait for her. With heavy steps, I start back down the driveway.

"Not leaving so soon, are you, Gabby Girl?" my father calls into the falling night. "You are so close."

Chapter 25

GABBY

I freeze in shock. He saw us. He knew we were here. Slowly I turn around and face the house. He is standing on the crumbling front step. Even in the dark, I can see the gun in his hand.

"You going to shoot us?" I shout across the yard. "We're not armed."

"Nice sticks," he says sarcastically.

I toss my stick into the woods. Lacey tosses hers too. "Now we aren't"

"Fine. Have it your way." He sets the gun on the step and raises his hands to show they are empty. "Now come on up here and let's talk like civilized people."

"Is Aubry okay?" Lacey asks as we slowly make our way towards the house.

"Wow, you're even prettier in person than you are on

TV. You look like your mom."

"Aubry? Where is she?" Lacey pushes.

"She's inside, feeling no pain thanks to what Drummond gave her. I fear he may have overdone it a bit."

"You drugged her?" I ask although I already know the answer.

"Easiest way to keep her quiet. That girl is feisty. Of course, she is my blood."

We've reached the steps and stand in front of him. Another mosquito is buzzing me, but I ignore it. "Now what?" I ask him. "Do we just stand here all night?"

"You tell me. You're the crime fighting hero."

"I'm not a hero."

"And I'm not the monster you think I am."

"Tell that to the dead guy we found earlier."

"You found him? Man, you are better than I thought." He fairly glows with pride. It makes me uncomfortable. "As for what we are doing now, the answer is up to you, Gabby. You can come join me and we'll escape leaving Aubry with Lacey safe and sound."

"Or?"

"Or," he suddenly reaches into the waistline at his back

and pulls a gun. "Or we can do this the hard way." Lacey and I both put our hands up.

Staring down the barrel of the gun, my answer is easy enough. If it will keep Lacey and Aubry safe, I'll do whatever I need to.

I drop my hands and take a step towards him. "If you promise to let Aubry and Lacey go, I'll do whatever you ask."

"Finally," he says, keeping the gun trained on my chest. "I knew you'd eventually realize you were more like me than like Emily. I guess Grandma Dot didn't ruin you after all." He lowers the gun and reaches for my bare hand. Luckily it's my right, but his touch makes my skin crawl just the same. "We have a lot to discuss," he says. "I need to get out of the country and you can help me. We'll go together. How does Costa Rica sound?"

I've always wanted to go to Costa Rica, but not with him. I swallow hard and wrack my brain for a way out of this. I can't imagine a life on the run with him, using what God blessed me with for evil.

Once the immediate threat to her is gone, Lacey bolts for the front door calling to her sister.

"You'll really let them go? Even without the ransom

money?" I ask.

He places the hand with the gun over his heart and squeezes my hand. "On my honor."

"You don't have any honor."

"Ouch. You'll see."

Lacey had torn open the door and entered the house. Drummond is yelling, telling her to get out or else.

"Let them go, Drummond or meet the same fate as Rogers."

Drummond shuts up. Lacey is murmuring to Aubry. I pull my hand from his grip and step into the house, all too aware that he still holds a gun and not trusting him one bit.

Aubry is spread out on a mattress, thankfully fully clothed. Lacey is holding her head, trying to wake her up.

"What's wrong with her?" I ask Nathan.

"I told you, Drummond gave her a bit too much."

"I just did what you said," Drummond protests from the corner where he is watching. "You just going to let her go? What about the money you promised me?"

Nathan lifts the gun and shoots the man in the chest.

Lacey screams and I jump. "What? Why?" I ask, turning on my father in anger.

"Just tying up some loose ends before we leave," he says. The glint in his eyes proves what I already feared. I made a deal with the devil.

Lacey is horrified and begins to sniffle. "Get her out of here," I tell her. She wraps her arm under Aubry's shoulders and tries to lift her. "Come on, Aubry. I need your help here."

Aubry moans at being moved and her eyes flutter open. "Lacey? Is that really you?"

"Get your feet moving," Lacey demands. Aubry does her best to stand. Half-dragging her sister, Lacey pulls her towards the front door.

I wish I was going with them, but I watch helplessly as they exit the house into the night.

Nathan let's them go. Drummond moans, crumpled in the corner. He's silenced with another bullet.

Outside, I hear Lacey scream my name.

"I'm okay," I shout. "Just go."

Drummond is now silenced and I'm alone with the monster who gave me life.

"Have you enjoyed having a sister?" he asks casually. "Two sisters, actually. Not that you've spent any time with Aubry."

I don't know how to answer.

He continues, "She's lovely, by the way. Aubry is. We originally were going to take Lacey, but she's a bit of a wild card. Aubry is more gentle and easier to control."

"Why are you doing all this? Is it just a game to you? You killed Aubry's boyfriend and now your two helpers. Does killing mean nothing to you?"

He shrugs and it infuriates me. "All part of the job."

My skin crawls and I rub my arms. I wish my tattoo would tell me something, give me a clue as to how to get out of this mess. It's silent.

"So what do we do now?"

He looks out the window, moving the curtain with the tip of his gun. "Now we wait for your brother to show up. I know you had to have called them."

"What do you want with Dustin?" I ask, fear creeping in my belly.

"Another loose end. Then we have one more stop before we leave."

"Costa Rica?"

"Eventually. I have a big job we need to do first. I would have done it alone, but it will be much easier with you on the team."

"I'm flattered," I say with heavy sarcasm.

"You should be," he says, missing the sarcasm.

We wait in silence for a few minutes, him checking the window often.

"You know, you should be thanking me." He breaks the silence.

"How's that?"

"If it wasn't for me, you wouldn't have your gift." He touches his eyebrow. I reach up and touch mine, feel the familiar scar there.

"You nearly killed me and I should thank you?"

"I stayed long enough to make sure you were breathing. I knew you'd wake up eventually. Besides, if you had stayed in your bed like I planned I wouldn't have had to take you down."

"I was just a child."

He smiles coldly. "Even children can be liabilities."

He looks out the window again, puts his face close to the glass. "Cavalry is here. It's show time."

Before I can ask his plan, he grabs me by the hand and drags me out onto the porch. It's my left hand, the cut one, the gifted one.

And it's bare.

I can see his plan in his mind. Draw Dustin out and shoot him in cold blood.

"Even you wouldn't do that," I say disgusted.

"You saw that." He squeezes my hand tighter making the cut sting. Darkness swirls inside him, a deep anger and frustration that makes me nauseous with its intensity.

"Please let go," I beg. He drops my hand but keeps the gun pointed at me. My legs are weak and I struggle to hold myself up.

He crouches and retrieves the gun he left on the step earlier. With a gun in each hand, he yells to the shadows moving in the dark woods.

"Dustin, my boy, I know you are out there. Why don't you show yourself and we can talk?"

"You won't hurt Gabby?" my brother responds.

"I promise not to hurt her. Why would I now that she's agreed to help me."

A shadow separates itself from the deep dark of the woods. "What do you want to talk about."

Nathan points both guns.

"Dustin, run!" I scream.

Chapter 26

GABBY

As soon as I scream, a gunshot tears through the night. I see Dustin's shadow duck back into the cover of the woods. From the way he moves, I don't think he is hurt.

Nathan turns on me, anger a fire in his eyes. "Why did you do that?"

"Why do you think?" I raise my chin and meet his eyes, anger in my own. "I'm not going to stand here and let you shoot him in cold blood."

He advances on me, hands full of guns. I stand firm, don't cower.

"You will learn not to disobey," he hisses.

"You will learn you can't control me. No one can."

We stand on the steps, candle light from the window flickering across his face. That face suddenly breaks into a huge smile.

"That's my girl. I underestimated you."

I'm uncomfortable with his change of attitude, but at least Dustin is safe and so am I. For now.

"Drop the guns and step away from her," Dustin yells from the darkness.

"You're brother is such a pain. You sure you don't want me to hurt him?" he asks in a low voice.

"He might be useful later," I say playing along.

His eyes open in surprise. "Way to think ahead. Now, let's get out of here."

He suddenly throws his arm around my neck and pulls me to his chest. I can smell the gunpowder on the gun in his hand under my chin. The other gun is pressing against my temple.

A shot of fear rushes through me. He wouldn't actually hurt me after all this?

"I'm taking Gabby and leaving," he shouts to the woods. "Try to interfere and she dies."

He pushes the gun at my head so firmly against my skin I cry out in pain. He pulls me down the steps and around the side of the house.

I can sense the police surrounding the house, the S.W.A.T. team is out there. So is Lucas. I feel comforted knowing they are here.

But there's nothing they can do while he has a gun to my head. Nothing I can do either.

I pray for guidance from my tattoo, but it is curiously silent.

A small, dark car waits behind the house. A path is cut through the woods, probably an old drive that goes to the other side of the country block.

He opens the passenger door and pushes me into the seat. "One quick stop and we're gone. Now, don't try anything or I *will* shoot you."

At this point, I'm not sure if he's playing tough for the police's sake or if he really would pull the trigger.

I search the edge of the woods as he shuts the door. A familiar shape is nearby, behind a large tree in the back yard. I'd recognize that shape anywhere.

It's Lucas. And he's only ten feet away.

As Nathan rounds the car, a bullet sizzles by. Nathan screams.

I take advantage of the moment and throw the car door open. I make a mad sprint for the big tree, terrified I will be shot in the back.

My chest aches and I'm gasping for breath as I duck

behind the tree, but I'm whole and unhurt.

"Stay down," Lucas commands.

I sink to the ground and wrap my arms around my knees to make myself as small as possible.

I hear a car door shut and the engine start. Tires spin on gravel. Lucas shoots at the car, but it fades down the lane.

Lucas barks into the radio on his shoulder. "He's on a back lane, headed for Lincoln Rd. Get a unit over there."

His legs are so close, I can touch him. I long for him to crouch next to me, take me in his arms. Instead, he continues to stand and looks down at me. "You okay?"

I nod, adrenaline making me shake.

"Good." I watch as the legs walk away, taking a piece of my heart with them.

I push to my feet, not sure what to do. Dustin runs around the house, sees me at the tree and comes to me.

"You okay? He didn't hurt you, did he?" He holds me by the shoulders and looks me over.

"He almost shot you again," I say and lean against my brother's chest.

"But you didn't let him." He rubs my back awkwardly, an unusual gesture of concern.

I allow myself a moment of weakness then pull away. "Aubry?"

"She's drugged but unharmed. At least not physically. An ambulance is on the way to check her out and take her to the hospital to be safe."

"That's good. Is Lacey with her?"

"Yeah." Dustin shuffles his boots on the grass and I search behind him for Lucas, unable to stop myself. He reads my mind and the moment grows tense.

"I'm glad you came."

"I'm glad you called. We'll need a complete report of what happened here. Do you have any idea what his plans are?"

"He is trying to get to Costa Rica. At least that's what he said. Who knows what's the truth with him."

Another officer joins us, asking Dustin a question. I search for Lucas again, but I only see other officers.

"Ambulance is here," Officer Patterson says, joining our small group. "Do you need checked out, Gabby?" he asks.

I don't but I want to see for myself that Aubry and Lacey are safe.

Alone, I make my way around the house and towards

the bright lights of the ambulance. An EMT is checking Aubry over. She's a little more awake, but still very groggy.

Lacey sees me and reaches for my hand. "You did it. You saved her," she exclaims in excitement.

"But Nathan got away."

"But Aubry is safe," she counters.

I smile at both my sisters. "Just glad we're all safe." I shuffle my feet and my eyes are drawn to the milling officers, searching for Lucas. I see him near the house, his back to me.

My arm suddenly tingles. I listen, expecting a message like *go to him*.

Go home.

That's not what I want to hear.

Go home.

Insistent, demanding I obey.

"Are you going to ride with Aubry in the ambulance?" I ask Lacey.

She puts an arm around her sister. "I'm not letting her out of my sight."

"Can I take your car?"

Lacey's eyes widen in surprise. "Sure. Are you

leaving?"

"I can give my report later. I have to go home."

"Okay," she says confused.

"If Dustin asks, tell him I got a message that said 'Go Home'."

"You're just going to go?"

"Are your keys in the car?"

"They are. Gabby what's going on?"

"I'm not sure. Just tell Dustin 'go home.'"

I leave Lacey and the excitement of the crime scene behind and walk down the weed covered driveway. Bugs sing loudly and buzz my ears. I swat at them angrily. Anger. That's what I feel. First Nathan puts a gun to my head, then Lucas acts as if I don't exist.

I break into a run and pound my legs as hard as I can the rest of the way to Lacey's car. I pass a few officers that give me questioning looks, but I pound on.

Out of breath, I let myself into the driver's seat. The car smells of smoke and an empty Diet Coke can is in the cup holder. Being in her car without her feels oddly intimate.

I long for my Charger.

Go home.

"I am," I grumble. "Be patient."

I drive down the dark country roads away from the action across the street from Von Aries Kennels. "I should have made the connection earlier," I mutter, my anger now directed at myself.

Making turns without thinking, I find myself on Grandma Dot's road.

Go home.

Grandma Dot's is home.

I pull into the drive and park next to my Charger by the barn. The big sliding door is open a foot or two. I stare at the dark crack.

I know Mom and I shut it tight earlier.

Jet barks inside, insistent and fearful. Not his usual "someone's here" bark.

All my senses on alert, I climb out of the car and up the porch steps. When I let myself in the back door, Jet tries to dart out. I stop him and shut the door behind me.

"Grandma Dot?" I call into the house. Jet has stopped barking, but paws at the back door.

Besides the ruckus Jet is making, the house is quiet.

Music starts playing, making me jump. A phone is on the kitchen island, buzzing and singing. "Gabby's Shop" is on the ID.

I answer the phone with a slow, "Hello?"

"Gabby, is that you?" Mom asks. "So you're safe."

"Why are you calling from the shop?"

"Because that is my phone. I didn't know where I put it. I was calling it to see if I could hear it. Where are you? I don't see you here."

"I'm at Grandma's. You must have left it here."

"Oh," she sounds exasperated. "I thought it was here. I guess I'll have to drive over and get it."

"Mom, did Grandma go somewhere tonight? Is she out with Mrs. Mott or something?"

"She didn't mention it. Mrs. Mott left before I did. I'm guessing the search for Aubry didn't go well if you are back at Grandma's already."

"I don't want to go into it right now, but we found her."

"That's wonderful. Why do you sound so sad about it?"

"A lot happened. Look, Grandma isn't here. Unless she went to bed already, but then Jet would be with her," I muse. Jet is still scratching to be let out and whining. "Okay, Jet, give me a minute." He looks my way expectantly.

"I'll be right over," Mom says. "I'm sure she's fine."

I hang up and let Jet outside. Instead of running for the grass to do his business, he runs directly to the open barn door.

"Jet, you don't need to go in there," I say as I follow. The memory of the raccoons in the barn fresh after our encounter this morning, I worry a tiny dog like Jet might get attacked.

The door is open just enough to fit through. I take a step inside, calling for the dog.

I remember the light switch to my left and flip it on. A dark, sick feeling comes up my bare fingers as I touch the switch.

The single bulb in the ceiling doesn't give much light but I can see Grandma Dot tied to a chair.

Chapter 27

GABBY

"I told you I had one more stop, one more loose end to clean up before I left," Nathan says, leaning against a wall in shadow.

Grandma's eyes are huge with fear and anger. A rag is shoved into her mouth. She makes a frustrated sound and wriggles against the zip ties holding her bound to the chair. Jet paws at her bare feet, anxious.

"Crazy old woman never did like me. I tolerated her for years. Mostly for your sake. Emily thought it was important you had a close relationship with her mother. I wanted to get rid of her the whole time."

"So why tie her up? You could have just shot her and been done with it."

"This is more fun. I had a feeling you'd show up here eventually. You always do." I don't like that he can guess my movements so easily. "Of course, I figured it would be a while yet. I barely had time to secure the zip ties before you pulled in. Didn't want to stick around with our boyfriend?"

I'm ashamed to feel my face burn. I turn away from him but not before he sees my reaction.

"Oh, trouble in paradise? Yeah, love sucks."

"But you are doing this because you love Jenna."

"I was hurting Anthony because of Jenna. This," he points the gun at Grandma, "I do because you betrayed me tonight."

I step forward, afraid he'll pull the trigger. Grandma wriggles again, but the ties hold fast.

"If you're mad at me, take me. Leave her out of it."

"But I'm enjoying this," he says smugly. "Next you're going to offer to join me and let her go."

"Will it work?"

I wish I had a gun, wish I had backup. I wish Grandma was safe in her bed.

He steps closer to her and runs the barrel of the gun down her cheek. Jet barks at him.

He points the gun at the dog and takes aim. "Shut up you stupid thing."

His finger moves on the trigger.

"Don't!" I rush him barrel into his chest. The gun shoots at the roof of the barn as he falls.

Jet continues barking, unaware of how close he came to being shot.

Nathan lands on his back and I jump onto his chest, pounding him with my fists. Jet attacks his face and sinks his teeth into an ear. While he's distracted by the dog bite, I wrestle the gun from his grasp. Once the heavy weapon is in my hands I point it at his head.

"Jet, get back," I command. Jet runs to Grandma's side and bares his teeth.

Blood seeps from the tiny punctures Jet gave him. He wipes at his ear, moving slowly. He touches his ear then looks at the blood on his fingers. "The little mutt bit me."

"You tried to shoot him. Who shoots a defenseless dog."

He holds his torn ear. "Look what he did to me. I don't call him defenseless."

I don't like the feel of him under me, so close. Keeping the gun trained on him, I remove myself from his chest and stand up. I'm aware he has another gun somewhere. He may have left it in the car, but I expect it is hidden on him. I begin to pat him down, feeling for the weapon.

He lies on his back. With the gun pointed at him, he has to let me look. He laughs. "You act like a cop."

"Don't laugh at me," I pat down one leg paying close attention to his ankle where he might have a hidden holster. That leg is clean.

I'm about to check the other leg when a car pulls in. Grandma makes a noise against the gag.

"That's probably the police," I bluff. It's possible Dustin got the message, but I doubt he'd be here already with a crime scene and another dead body to deal with.

Jet runs out of the barn. "Jet, what are you doing out here alone?" Mom asks.

Mom. I'd forgotten she was coming to get her phone.

Grandma makes a noise of warning against the gag.

"What the-?" Mom says and I hear gravel crunching, growing closer.

"Mom, get out of here and call the police," I shout over my shoulder.

Mom appears in the slightly open door. "Oh my. Nathan?"

He takes advantage of the small distraction and kicks the gun from my hand. Before I can recover, he disappears into the looming shadows of the huge barn.

Mom hurries to Grandma and pulls the gag out of her mouth. "That man attacked me in my bed," she says as soon as she can. "Who attacks an old woman in her bed?"

"Are you okay?" Mom asks.

"I will be once you cut me from this chair." Grandma wriggles and the chair scratches against the concrete of the floor. "Where did he go, Gabriella?"

The barn creaks and some hay rustles in the loft. "I think he went up there." I search for the gun he kicked away then point the retrieved gun at the dark hay loft.

Mom is moving things about on the work bench, frantically looking for something. "Found them," she says and turns with some wire cutters in her hand. Soon Grandma's ties are all cut loose. She jumps out of the chair and rubs her wrists. Her long flowered night gown blows around her ankles. "Oh my, I'm out here in my night gown," she mutters and picks up Jet. "It's okay, baby. Momma's okay," she coos to the dog.

"What are we going to do?" Mom says quietly. I feel like I've been asked that question a lot lately. I don't know. What would Lucas or Dustin do in this situation?

Wait for back up.

Forget that.

Another rustling sound from the loft. I'm pretty sure he's up there. "Mom, you take Grandma inside and call for backup. I'm going up after him."

"But that's dangerous," Grandma protests.

"I don't care, he's gone too far this time, coming after you. He might have another gun. He had one earlier. You two go inside where it's safe," I command.

Grandma puts Jet down and picks up a shovel. "Not a chance." She looks quite a sight in her nightgown holding shovel, murder in her eyes.

"Me, too," Mom says and finds a rake.

Laughter suddenly echoes through the barn, coming from the loft.

"You three look ridiculous," Nathan says. He steps into a shaft of light from the bulb at the top of the barn. He has the missing gun in hand. "A shovel and a rake against this?" He laughs again. "I could have shot you and you wouldn't even have seen it coming."

Mom and Grandma duck behind some crates, away from the pointed gun.

The Kubota tractor is between me and the ladder to the loft. I make my way around it, the gun in my hand trained on him. I skirt the blades of the tiller attached to the back of the tractor. It's a tight fit and I scratch my leg on the blade.

"Crap on a cracker," I mutter at the pain, but I keep the gun on Nathan.

"You coming up, Gabby Girl? We going to have a shoot off?"

I reach the ladder to the loft. In order to climb up, I need both hands. Hoping he doesn't shoot, knowing the angle is bad for him to aim at me, I tuck the gun in the back of my pants and climb as fast as I can to the loft.

He waits for me in the shadows, seems to be enjoying the action. "This is more fun than I've had in months."

"You've been in jail for months," I point out, taking the gun from my waistband. It shakes slightly in my hand.

"Exactly," he says, suddenly serious, his voice an evil hiss. "And whose fault is that?"

"Yours." I say with forced bravado.

"No. It's your fault." His gun is suddenly pointed straight at me.

I raise the heavy pistol and point it at him. My palms grow slick with sweat and I grip tight to keep it steady.

"Since you won't join me, I only have one option," he

explains. He takes a slow step towards me. I resist the urge to step back from him. "You won't stop until you get me behind bars again."

"That's right." My tattoo finally starts to tingle, I welcome the welcome the guidance and listen intently. "So give up now."

He laughs. "Nice try."

Shoot the hay.

I don't waste time questioning, I point the gun at the hay bale nearest his head and pull the trigger. The recoil of the gun knocks me back.

Nathan rushes forward.

A blur of gray springs from behind the bale disturbed and scared by my shot.

A raccoon.

It jumps onto Nathan, scratching his face, tearing at his hair. The raccoon squalls a horrible noise and sinks his teeth into the already bitten ear.

Nathan drops the gun and fights the coon. He holds it with both hands and pulls, screaming along with the animal. He spins around, trying to get loose.

The edge of the loft is inches from his feet when he loses balance.

I think he's going to win the fight against gravity, but, in slow motion, he falls off the loft.

His body lands on the tiller below with a sickening sound. I rush to the edge just in time to see the raccoon run away and out the door.

Nathan is impaled on the blades of the tiller. He looks up at me and meets my eyes. For a moment, I see the man that I knew as a child.

"It hurts," he says, no longer the brash crime boss. Just a man. An injured man.

Mom and Grandma hurry around the tractor to him, rake and shovel still in hand and held at the ready.

He rolls sideways, pulling himself off the tiller. Grandma grips the shovel tighter, ready to do battle if needed. Nathan collapses on the floor at their feet.

He's alive, but his back is bleeding and soaking his shirt.

Mom's mouth is open in shock and Grandma toes his body, making sure he's really down.

"This is for what you've done to my family." Grandma twists up her mouth and spits on him.

Nathan makes a sound half laugh and half moan as he wipes the spit from his face. "You old bag."

"Don't talk to my mom like that." Mom kicks him in the ribs and he moans loudly.

He rolls onto his side, tries to get up.

Mom and Grandma raise their weapons, ready to battle.

He slumps back to the floor and his eyes flutter and close. He looks unimpressive covered in blood and spit and slumped on the ground. Nothing like the monster he is inside.

"Is he dead?" Grandma looks to me for an answer.

I hurry down the ladder and join them at this side. I kneel next to his body and touch his chest with my left hand.

The sickening darkness fills me. So does the will to live.

"He'll be okay," I say. "He'll survive."

"Too bad," Mom says.

"Emily," Grandma admonishes. "We don't wish death on anyone. Not even him. God wouldn't like it."

Mom is saved from further lecture by the squeal of the heavy barn door against the track as it's pulled open.

"Gabby?" Dustin calls. "Are you in here?"

"We're over here."

Dustin makes his way around the tractor and finds the three of us staring at Nathan's unmoving body.

He looks at Nathan then at me with questions in his eyes.

"He'll make it. He's hurt, but not fatally."

"Not sure how I feel about that after what he's done," he says.

"We'll let the court take care of it," I say. "You must have gotten my message from Lacey."

Dustin shakes his head. "I didn't talk to Lacey. Lucas knew to come."

"Lucas is here?" My heart picks up its pace and I search the barn for his familiar form.

Then I see him, lurking in the doorway of the barn. His blue eyes find mine and we stare at each other for a long moment. He nods sadly and turns away.

His feet crunch the gravel as he walks to his car. My hear breaks as I hear his engine start and he drives away.

I want to chase after him. I want to tell him I'm sorry, that it's all been a bad mistake. I want things to go back to how they were.

I walk to the door of the barn and watch his taillights disappear over a hill. Grandma is suddenly by my side.

"Go to him. We can handle this here."

I take two steps towards my Charger when my arm tingles.

Stay.

I turn back to the barn.

As always, I obey.

THE END

If you love the Gabby books, keep your eye out for the next one coming in summer of 2022.

Until then, you might enjoy the first book in the Harper Lakes Murder Thrillers series, "Water for Murder"

Water for Murder: Kenda is starting her life over in her home town on the Harper Lakes Chain when she gets sucked into a murder investigation that hits close to her heart. With some help from the ghost of her dad, she must solve the mystery or die trying. Fun on the lakes and a twisty mystery. Enjoy it today.

A note from the author:

Wow this book took me a long time and caused a lot of angst. I started this book not long after I published Message in the Box. That was eight months ago. I wrote the first chapters, then got stuck. I just couldn't get into the story.

So I switched gears and wrote "The Moon has a Name" instead.

Back to Gabby and I forced a few more chapters out. This was supposed to be the final Gabby book and wrap up the series. I needed it to be really good. Instead I couldn't figure out who the kidnapper was. (an important detail haha).

So I tried for a few weeks and made a little progress. Then I had a great and shiny new idea and took another detour and wrote "13 Doors."

Then back to Gabby again. I planned to end the series as I have other projects I wanted to work on. I was honestly a bit burned out on Gabby after five previous books and wanted to write darker books like Moon and Doors were. I tried and tried to wrap everything up in one last book.

But Gabby wouldn't talk to me. I could get into the other character's heads, but not hers. So I kept toiling a chapter here and a chapter there. All the while, I whined to my family and friends that the book just wasn't working. I'd post to the fan club about my "progress" or lack of. One of my posts I said how hard it was to get Gabby to talk to me for this final book. One of the members commented that maybe Gabby didn't want this to be her last book.

Then it hit me. She didn't want it to end and neither did I. I literally talked to my husband about it one tear filled morning when I was complaining about how hard the book was to work on. It was a revelation to me. I didn't want it to be the last!

And Gabby started talking. If finished the last half of this book in a three day binge of writing. I wrote so much my hands and arms literally ached from typing. I loved it! I just sat down and let the words come. I had a rough idea of where I was headed, but I let Gabby lead. She's stubborn and does what she wants anyway.

Sometimes even I didn't know why she did things, I just trusted God that it would all work out. Like when Lacey knocks on the door at Gabby's house. I wrote about the knock then sat back and said to my office "Who is there?" Turns out it was Lacey and off they went. When the raccoon jumps at them in the old house, I didn't understand why there was something as random as a raccoon in the story. Turns out it was to come back up in a big way later. It is strange, this gift God gave to me. He drives and I just write what he wants me to. This was a wild ride.

And here we are, all done and published.

I truly hope you loved this book as much as I loved writing the last half of it. Gabby will have a few more adventures to come. I don't make any promises, but if she has a story she wants told, I will tell it.

I hope to have the next book out as soon as possible. By the time this book is published, I will have already started on the new one.

Thank you for being such a loyal reader and going along with Gabby's adventures with me. Thank you for being so patient if you waited on this book. I have said many times, I have the best readers in the world. Join my fan club and say hi. I'd love to meet you.

God Bless,

Dawn Merriman

Printed in Great Britain
by Amazon